DAN

DAN

by

Kenneth C Steven

SCOTTISH CULTURAL PRESS

First published 1994

Scottish Cultural Press
PO Box 106
Aberdeen AB9 8ZE
Scotland
Tel/Fax: 0224 583777

The publisher acknowledges subsidy from the Scottish
Arts Council towards the publication
of this volume

British Library Cataloguing in Publication Data
A CIP catalogue record for this book is available from the British
Library

ISBN: 1 898218 07 2

Printed and bound by
Athenaeum Press Ltd, Newcastle upon Tyne

For Donald Stewart
of Croftgarrow

and to remember Lexie Walker –
the last Gaelic speaker of Glen Lyon

ACKNOWLEDGEMENTS

The irony is that *Dan* was not written in Northern Scotland at all, but rather in Arctic Norway during the winter of 1991. Perhaps there are times when it is easier to see one's own country and people through a telescope than a window.

I want to thank Angus and Irene Howat especially for their tremendous encouragement and assistance in getting the novel published. Sincere thanks are also due to those who read and evaluated the typescript with such patience, not least my father and mother.

The publisher acknowledges with thanks the permission granted by C Macdonald of *Runrig*, to use the words of 'Dust' in the foreword.

DUST

So lead me to the river
Blood runs thicker than the water

Wrap me in your sheets together
Where my earth heart lies forever

No they can't understand
The hole that is in my heart

I've lived my life here with the others
I long to live with you my brothers

And my drum will beat this day
Pounding for the Gael

An end to sighs, all hands unite
In the spring that lies behind this sorrow

Deep the faith and pure the light
That shines inside and guides your people

Oh I do believe
Dust will turn the seed
Home

C Macdonald

Chapter 1

It was thawing. He could tell that even before he got up that morning, before he had made his way to the window to let the light in. There was a thrush singing, the notes thick and rich as blood. He could hear Kate out in the yard behind the house, her feet going through slush. And then the drops from the window, chimes of bright water.

He would not get up yet. He lay still, looking around him at the familiar room. On the chest of drawers, beyond the thin layer of dust, he could see the faded photograph of his mother and father - the tall dark man, unsmiling, his black coat tightly buttoned; his mother, still young, her head tilted slightly, her hands folded, curved as though they might have been holding a young bird. That was before his older brother had been born, he mused - Andrew, the boy who had gone to France to be killed. And then the picture of Andrew himself, in uniform. The boy's moustache, the lean, intelligent face with its high cheekbones, the woman's hands. He had been killed in 1918, one week before war's end.

He could see the clock, still keeping its steady time. It brought back vivid memories of his grandfather, Alan, who had been in this glen and this farm before them all. He could see his face so clearly, with a silver beard, as he took him out as a little boy to see the horses. That clock had been on the mantelpiece then, above the open fire; it was shaped like a sphinx and had mahogany shoulders.

Suddenly the sun came into the room, between the faded curtains which did not meet. He wanted to be up, to see the fields and hills now that the fresh green of spring was being reborn; the unexpected fall of snow had not lasted long. Still he did not get up. The room was a protection, a place that was his own, that did not change like the road which had been the bringer-in of a new world with strange ways. In this room Dan had been born, and here his mother had died. It was also the room

1

that he and Catriona had shared for so many years. All of them were together, it now seemed to him, their ghosts in the separate compartments of his mind, like the clean drawers of the chest itself. They were now both comfort and nightmare; they were as naked white hands beneath the weakness of his old age, supporting him although they could no longer speak.

He must get up. He heard Rory barking in the yard, and imagined him bouncing around Kate as she came back from the sheep. There was the creaking of the back door and the sound of her steps. He sat up, reached for his mother's old hand mirror and looked at himself; there were red flecks about the edges of his eyes. For a moment Dan was vividly aware of Catriona; it was as though he could feel her hands on the wooden edges of his shoulders, her warm breath on his cheek; but then she was gone, the moment of remembering past. He shuddered and pulled back the heavy old homespun blankets, his hands foolish and stumbling with their blue veins of cold. It took him a long time to get dressed, to draw the thick trousers over the pathetic thinness of his legs; he felt sharp needles in his arms as he drew the sweater over his head.

A faint sound of fluttering drew his attention to the window. He went over to draw back the curtains and saw the butterfly, a tortoiseshell. Its wings were still slow and heavy after winter sleep, and it did not attempt to escape as the old man held out his forefinger and let it settle. The sun, coming down in folds from the side of Beinn Dobhran, spilled on to his hand, lighting the chain of blue lacing on the edges of its wings. Suddenly a memory came back of the last summer before his brother had left for France; Dan had been five then, just old enough for his brother to take him and show him things of wonder in the fields and woods around the farm - deep exciting caves, trees where squirrels were often to be seen, big pools in the river where salmon came, butterflies in the fields' edges. He still recalled how he had tried to catch a butterfly, and how his frustration

2

grew as it repeatedly flew further away at his approach; and Andrew had laughed as he had forgotten to look where he was going and had fallen into a shallow ditch, howling with pain and rage.

That memory sparked off another. One day he had been sailing a toy boat on the small pond; Andrew came and knelt beside him.

'A present for you, Danny,' he had said, with more than usual gentleness.

'What is it?' Dan had replied, not looking up, so absorbed was he in the progress of his boat.

His brother for reply dropped a parcel on the ground beside him. Inside were toy sheep, cows and hens. He could still recall how, although he had said his thanks as he had been taught, his disappointment had shown; he had felt himself to have grown past such childish things. He had immediately turned back to his boat, and hardly looked up as his brother said goodbye and started walking down the track. Only much later did he understand the meaning of the gift - when he found on his father's desk the paper, with its message so simply written that it sounded almost harsh:

'I want you to know, father, that Danny is to take over the farm instead of me. Whatever happens while I am in France, I do not want you to think that I will one day be master of Achnagreine. If I come back, I will find a way to get to university and become a teacher. That is what I want.'

But what did all that mean to him as a young boy? Just as long as he was free to roam the woods, to find birds' nests in the spring and chestnuts and hazel nuts in the autumn, to watch fish in the pools and - if he was lucky enough - occasionally otters at play on the river bank, he was content. Day and night were one, that long summer before school began - the world of the farm was warm with his mother, and beyond the back door stretched eternity.

For a while, though, it seemed as if the skies were black without Andrew; but soon the time of the chestnuts came and he forgot.

The butterfly dipped its wings on the old man's hand and suddenly flew away. Dan opened the window and gently guided the fragile creature to its edge, watching as it rose like a red leaf into the sunlight and was lost to view. He went out of the room and descended the wooden staircase with slow and painful steps; at the foot, he stopped and looked up at the three paintings which his mother had done during her last illness - geese in the field south of Achnagreine, with the long line of elms behind; the view west to Beinn Dobhran in autumn; and the fallow field running down to the ruins of the old Lodge. He could see her still, painting that last canvas in her room, could visualise so clearly the pale oval of her face and the sensitive artist's hands. She would not allow him to look until she had finished. The work had taken her a long time.

Rory had heard him coming down. Dan had tried to be quiet so that Kate would not hear him; but now the collie came padding out of the kitchen and thrust his wet nose into the old man's hand. He looked down into the wise eyes and whispered to him in Gaelic; then they went in together to where Kate was working at the range. There was a smell of fresh baking; she had put wood on the fire and flames leaped up like sleek wolfhounds. Rory lay down on the sheepskin rug, his head on his paws, the blue eyes looking warily at Kate.

'And what are you doing there, dog?' she said sharply. 'You're getting soft too young.'

'Ach, let him lie,' Dan answered her gently as he came over to the warmth of the fire. She didn't turn towards him; she was lifting a heavy pan on to the edge of the sink.

'I'm . . . I'm thinking of going up to Beinn Dobhran today,' he heard himself say; the statement had an air of uncertainty which he immediately regretted.

'What, now?' she answered loudly. He saw that she had tied back her long straight hair and that it was beginning to grey. 'Rory! Will you go out when you're told!' There was an edge to her voice now. She left the sink and came over to the old man, wiping her hands on her apron. Rory slunk off to the back door and thumped down with a heavy sigh. 'You must be out of your mind, even thinking of going out on a day like this!,' she continued. 'One slip on this slush and you'll land somewhere none of us may be able to find you.'

He felt his cheeks beginning to redden. Treating him like a child again! He put out a hand to the mantelpiece to steady himself; he could feel his heart starting to thud. 'I'll not be gone all that long,' he defended himself weakly. 'And there's plenty of light in the day...' his voice trailed away. 'There's one or two things I want to see before...'

'Before what?' she demanded.

'Am I a prisoner in my own house?' he exclaimed in sudden anger, stretching himself to his full height from where he had been leaning against the fireplace. He noted that even so she was still almost as tall as himself.

'Surely you can understand perfectly well why I'm concerned,' she now said in a gentler tone, turning back to the range and lifting the heavy kettle which was blowing a thin mist of steam. 'There are still plenty of drifts higher up that haven't melted yet, and who knows what might happen to you? But of course if you've set your mind to go I can't stop you. Anyway, at least have your porridge first.'

He sat down heavily at the table and she brought over his steaming bowl of porridge, which he ate in the time-honoured way, dipping each spoonful into a cup of creamy milk so that the porridge remained hot. He finished it and looked up at her.

'Right then, I'll be off.'

She returned his look, her expression kindly, almost but not quite smiling. Then he rose and went out without another word.

Chapter 2

At the very door the cold seemed to strike him. There was a wind coming from the north, and he went back into the porch to find his warm mitts and his shepherd's crook. The door made the same creak as it had done for as long as he could remember; even now he could hear it as he had long ago when his father went out in the early dark to the lambing. It had been a good feeling then, as he lay cosily in the sanctuary of his nest, imagining the cold outside, the studs of frost stars on the blue-black cloth of the sky, and the snow lying in thin ridges like watching wolves. Glad to be inside, yet wishing for the exultation of the fierce outdoors. But soon he would go back to sleep.

He did not take Rory. In fact the collie showed no sign of wanting to go with him, which was unusual, although Dan reckoned he was glad enough to be nearer the fire after a long spell at the sheep with Kate. He heard the river at once; fuller now than it had been for months, a deep booming as it charged through the gorge. That had been his favourite haunt when school was over. He would come in, breathless after running, to find his mother and wolf his tea and scones; then he would be off, running through the yard, over the field, then scrambling down to the river. Once he had found a deep black cairn-gorm pebble in one of the pools, smooth and rounded, and when he held it up to the light it had seemed hollow, its heart as if on fire. And when the river was low again, spring past with water coming down over the falls like little more than spittle over a bearded chin, he would go down to Donnie's Pool, the one he knew best of all, to guddle for trout. Andrew had given him his first lessons in the art that last summer before he left; when he did not come back, Angus from further up the glen, Andrew's great friend, continued to teach him until he knew every inch of the pool's edge, every bank where fish would be lying. Sometimes he would be nearly driven mad by the midges; they would swarm in a misty cloud around his head on a summer's evening; or his hands would be numb with cold, and hunger would gnaw at his stomach. But something would always draw him back again. As he leant out of his window late at night, long after he should have been asleep, a sudden thumping would begin in his heart and sweat would break out on his palms. Then stealthily he would open his window inch by inch, terrified lest his father might come upstairs; and soon he was free, out into the cool night and away down to the river.

Only once had he been caught, and the memory still had the power to make his heart beat faster. His father had been waiting for him as he came creeping in; a lamp blazed in his face.

'And what's the meaning of this?'

It was the deadly quietness of the voice that had appalled Dan. Far more deadly than shouting.

'I . . . I got a fish, dad...' The trout was torn out of hands.

'Don't ever dare to trick us like that again. Andrew never behaved like this! And do you know, boy, what day this is?'

The question had seemed to hang quivering in the air.

'Answer me.'

'The . . . the Sabbath, dad. I forgot.'

'You forgot! The Sabbath. Breaking God's holy law, the fourth commandment, the day of rest. Have you no shame, after all you have been taught?'

Dan stood there silent, feeling his lip begin to tremble, the tears ready to flow.

'You'll go to your bed now and you'll pray for forgiveness. Remember this - turn back from God too often and the door will close; you will be cast out. You have shamed this house today!'

Dan had held back the tears till he reached the safety of his room. Then huge sobs had torn him as he pressed his face deep into the pillow. 'Please Lord, forgive. Oh please, Lord Jesus, do not cast me out!' It was a long time before peace came to him and he slept that night.

Now the old man turned on the path towards the river and looked far down the glen. More memories, far more vivid than those of last year's events, came flooding back. Somewhere around the folds of the hills stood the church, by the village of Drumbeg. Each Sabbath they had marched there, he chafing against the stiffness of his best clothes, longing to be free to search for nests, to pick flowers, to climb trees. There was always so much to see - the high floating of an eagle, perhaps, as it sailed out wooden and straight from the high Corrie of Ben Dobhran; a heron at its fishing by the river bank - he had to make do with these pleasures. Sometimes it would be raining and he would find the going hard, and there was nothing to do but follow endlessly the stride of his father in front of him; it had seemed like a relentless march that would never end. Then it was a relief to reach the sanctuary of the church, to hear the drumming of the rain on the roof while he nestled close to his mother on the hard bench, growing warm again. He would always remember one window which was his great comfort. It was of stained glass, and showed Jesus holding a small boy in his arms. Later he had realised that there had been much controversy before it had been accepted by the elders; it was a gift from the laird, disapproved of by some because the churches of the time were severely plain and un-adorned. But in the end the more liberal faction had won. When he learned about this, how glad he was that they had! Underneath the picture were the simple words: 'Suffer the little children to come unto me.'

When the long, long sermon was about to begin, there would always be a peppermint to suck, pressed into his hand by one of the old women, a tide of rustling passing around the pews. And when he trembled to hear the stern old minister warn the congregation of judgement to come, his eyes would turn at once to that one window with its message, and find solace in seeing the gentle face of Christ, fancying that He was looking down at him; he would imagine himself the small boy held in the arms of the One who was a friend of fishermen - after all he, Danny, was a fisherman too. Somehow he felt that Jesus would be happy to come with him to the river, to see the pools where the salmon lay.

Thinking of the river always sent his mind wandering to his next fishing trip; soon he would go further afield, to explore new pools that he had never yet reached, far up on the shoulder of Beinn Dobhran. He would go to-morrow, after school! The peppermint burned in the corner of his cheek until it was away to nothing. He be-came restless and shifted endlessly on the hard seat. He looked along at his father; he seemed carved out of stone, his face stern and pale, his eyes fixed resolutely on the old man in the pulpit. Sometimes his mother would slip her opal brooch to him, the one that had been her own mother's; he would then sit with bowed head holding the thin bar of gold with its single oval stone, fascinated by the colours, blue and orange and red, as he turned it in the light.

At last the sermon was over and the last psalm sung. There would be a low murmur of voices as the congrega-tion pressed out through the door, shaking hands solemnly with the minister and gathering in sober groups. He would see other children there, looking as uncomfortable in their stiff clothes as he felt in his. Al-though the boys were intensely aware of the girls and eyed them covertly, they never spoke to them; except one day, he recalled, when his parents were deep in conver-sation with the parents of Jean MacBride, and he was told to walk along the road with her until they were ready. He never could stand Jean; she had a pernickety manner, and stood with her nose in the air talking to two of her elderly aunts who looked, he thought, like crows in their black shawls and long black skirts. Jean always wore the same white dress on summer Sundays along with a white hat with pink bows. Suddenly overcome by devilment, he could not resist walking behind her as they rounded the first bend, grabbing a large stone and lashing it down into one of the muddy pools she had just passed so that an arc of black drops splashed her back and bottom. She screamed with rage and tried to kick him, then burst into angry tears and ran back to the grown-ups while he choked with laughter. It was worth the thrashing he received.

Once the memories had been unleashed, it seemed as if they came like a flood. Forgetful of the spring cold, the old man sat down on the bench in the yard and thought about his parents. From an early age he had been conscious of the differences between them, his father's sternness in even sharper contrast because of his mother's extreme gentleness. There was just no hardness in her at all, he mused. And it was especially in the matter of their religious faith that the difference came to a head - his father a good man, honest to a fault, yet always aware of the necessity to keep the rules. Like the old minister - putting fear into your heart, telling you about the judgement to come. There was kindness in his father, though; yet Dan could not recall neighbours coming to him in trouble. With his mother, now, it was different; people made for her door in times of need - never a sick-bed for miles around but she would be there. She too had had a strong faith, but she did not talk about it much. It showed in all she did.

It was on those Sabbaths long ago that he had become aware of these things, he thought. He remembered the seemingly interminable afternoons, when he would have to sit in the parlour, with the choice of either Bunyan's *Pilgrim's Progress* or the Bible. He much preferred the Bible; the *Pilgrim's Progress* put the fear of death on him. The smell of that front room came back to him now. It was damp and fusty, used only on Sundays and special days like New Year; and he would sit as near the window as he could, to smell instead the flowers his mother would have put there - hyacinths in spring, lilac perhaps in summer, strongly scented flowers as if she too wanted to drown the fustiness. The river would be shouting for him to come; it often seemed like some terrible conspiracy that the skies should be clearer than usual, the world outside more than ever filled with waiting treasure. Never did the hands of the clock move more slowly than on Sabbath afternoons.

But then the whole aspect of the day would change. At five o'clock precisely, his father would leave the house, to begin the long tramp back again for the evening service. It seemed to Dan as if a dark shadow had been removed; his mother would build up the fire, and they would sit beside it in happy and relaxed companionship. When the flames had died down, leaving a glowing red heart, she would bring down the long brass toasting fork from its hook by the mantelpiece and leave him with slices of bread to toast, while she fetched the rest of their supper - milk, oatcakes with cheese or honey, and a banana, a great treat in those days - and spread butter on the hot toast where it melted in golden pools, and it was soft and hot in his mouth.

Often he begged his mother to tell him stories about the old days, when she was a child; he drank in all she said, asking endless questions. Or she would read him a story. Afterwards he would lie in bed cocooned in warmth and utter contentment; and long before his father returned he would be asleep.

What he certainly recognised in his mother was a kind of underlying sadness. Sometimes he would hear her crying upstairs after an exchange with his father; and he would tiptoe upstairs and listen quietly outside their door until he had summoned up enough courage to knock. But she never answered. An hour or so after he would find her down at the kitchen stove once more, singing softly to herself, turning to him with her gentle smile, with only the tell-tale edges of red about her eyes.

Dan now became aware of the cold and moved over towards the last of the barns. The river was louder; he could see a white tail of it higher up, reminding him of the scut of a rabbit as the water bounced down with its load of snow. There was time to go inside for a moment.

He smelled that warm darkness which he loved. The wooden door closed with a soft knock; a little light came from underneath. Two skylights let in their own narrow shafts of silver, the thick air was filled with dust, and golden flecks of hay danced in the pillars that struck the damp floor. To his left, in a corner, a lamb bleated. It was in a little pen and he saw its black legs folded under the frail shivering body. Born just this morning, he guessed, and its mother had refused to accept it. Dan knelt down and stretched out his hand; the lamb tried to rise on trembling legs, bleating in expectation of a further bottle, then collapsed back into the corner, a black face turned towards Dan. He tickled the tight curls in the middle of its forehead and got up, feeling the strain in his knees. He looked around. The same bales of hay stacked here, the same air of secrecy, the same sense of sanctuary. How far back these feelings went! This was where he had come with Jess, he remembered, smiling inwardly. She had been so shy of him, so much in awe of his father. Her family had come from the very top of the glen, from Camus Lurgan. That second year at school he had seen her; it was as if something in her face caught him every time he looked at her and paralysed him. He could never find any words to say to her; afterwards he had kicked himself for his stupidity, and planned what he would say to her next time. Once, the day before he knew she was to be coming to Achnagreine, he had lain awake half the night, promising himself that this time would be different.

The next morning he had waited, trembling with nervousness, for a sight of her father's cart as the farmer made his way down to Abercree for the market. They had sat among the hay bales because she had not wanted to meet his father. He had brought out a bottle of his mother's best home-made lemonade, a special treat, and a plate of her shortbread; for the first time he felt at home with her, and chattered away about fishing, and about things that had been happening that week at the school. She had been sitting at right angles to him, he remembered, the light coming down from the skylight and striking her face, and suddenly, quite beside himself, he leaned forward and planted a loud kiss in the middle of her cheek. She turned to him bewildered, like a deer startled in a glade, then leapt up and was away in a flash through the barn door, which banged loudly behind her. Dismay overwhelmed him. What had he done wrong? That was what the other boys had told him they had done, and all seemed to have gone well enough for them.

He trailed disconsolately to school the following Monday and kept as far away from her as he could; but his eyes burned into her back and a mixture of longing and shame struggled inside him. She never came to Achnagreine again. Once his mother asked if he would like her to invite Jess for tea one Saturday, but he made excuses about all the work he had to do, and the subject was never brought up again.

How strange, he thought now, that her shadow was still there in the old barn after all these years. She had grown up into a beautiful, rather aloof woman, had married young and left the glen many a long year ago. He never heard what had become of her.

Now the barn was in sore need of repair. He saw the white chinks in the walls where the light came in like steel arrows. So much work to be done! It surged through him, the longing to begin all over again, to have everything in good working order, to have whole days ahead - aye, and months, and years - ready to be filled with satisfying hard work. If he only had the time, and the strength! Time ran like water, now, through his hands. He could not bear to think of it. Leaving this beautiful world that was his. And yet, what did he have here any more? Memories surged back of days that were past, when he would come to this barn tired and broken at the day's end, to hang tools on their hooks before that final walk home into the golden light of the kitchen and the warmth of the fire - and Catriona. Sometimes before leaving the barn he would look up through the skylight at the jagged edges of the stars with their golden and red fires, or the light of the moon as it etched white cornices on Beinn Dobhran's sharp ridges. That sky was the same as it had always been, he thought now. The first man that came there and cut down the trees - began turning the earth to plant his poor seed - he too must have stood there and seen the same fragments of light burn in that sky, and the same haunting shoulders of the mountain lit up with rich mantles of moonbeams. It was as though they were kindred, separated by the long ages of time, yet somehow together, their hands on the same plough. They were born of the same earth, and in their veins was the sound of the same song. What he, Dan, did here would in a sense never be finished; they would come after him and stand in this place, their eyes drawn upward to the same sky. There were times he had almost felt their presence, as though their spirits somehow had been fused into one memory that lingered on, brushing occasionally against the world of his own day, as though re-visiting, remembering. Once, looking down from an upstairs room, he fancied he saw the half-bent back of a man ploughing, making a straight furrow in the field that ran down to the lodge. Only a moment and the figure was gone; drawing his hand over his eyes he saw only peewits making their ragged half-circles; weeping over the spring field. He said nothing to his mother; there were too many ghosts haunting her grey eyes already.

Three times in his life he had heard the crying of a woman in the small shed where he kept birch logs stacked for winter, three times so widely spaced through his life that he could not easily have told at what time of the year they had occurred. Wait, though - it was surely in those strange days between summer and autumn, days of a kind of waiting, when there was a stillness in the trees and fields, almost an unexplained anxiety. Dusk was coming earlier, yet the light hung blue and strange after the sun's fall and the hills were lit with a glow of ochre, unreal and tainted as if with blood. It was almost as though the glen strained with all its might against the chains that pulled onward into autumn, towards sleep

14

and the certainty of death. Each time, he had been coming up the path towards the house, weary and thinking
of nothing, hearing only the sound made by his feet as
they trod on the stones. And then, the muffled sound of
crying, as if the woman's hands covered her face. Each
time he went to the shed and opened the door as quietly
as he could; never was there anything to be seen. There
was the dark, deep smell of wood, but nothing else.

Chapter 3

He had gone at once to tell his grandmother about the crying that he had heard - Granny Drummond, wife of Alan, mother of John, his father, in whose hands Achnagreine now lay. Memories surged over him as he thought of her now - one of whose love he had been so sure always, who had time for him and would listen to his tales and share his joys and anxieties even when he seemed to be in the way of the others who were always so busy. Granny Drummond with her wrinkled, kind face; a face more than a little like a man's with its strong features and sometimes a half-frown which could give the impression of annoyance - until she smiled, and you were at once put at your ease. And when she spoke you caught the soft music of the Islands in her voice.

Looking back, Dan had often wondered why it was that no-one, not even his mother, had told him any of the things that he so much wanted to know about his grandparents. Why they so seldom came to Achnagreine, for example; they would come to the big family dinner at New Year, but hardly any other time. And they never seemed to want to stay long even then. It was only very gradually, as the years went past, that he came to know these things by himself - simply by listening, and asking questions, and then putting two and two together. About their attitude to his mother, for instance. They did not altogether approve of her, of that he was sure. Much later he understood why; it had to do with her painting pictures. Nobody in the glen ever thought of doing such a thing - least of all a woman. Artists occasionally came to the glen, and could be seen sitting with their easels painting Beinn Dobhran, perhaps, or a view of the river. But for working folk, painting was a frivolous thing, a waste of precious time; there was always so much else to be done. Only Dan knew how his mother worked to save the time for her art, how early she rose in the morning, how she set aside a single afternoon for it, and never another minute. It wasn't exactly a disgrace that she painted pictures - more of an embarrassment; not as if she, the wife of an elder, had worn trousers, or been seen smoking! These things were unheard-of.

Then there was the question of the farm. It gradually dawned on the boy that his grandparents came visiting so seldom partly because they just could not bear to see the place that had been their own home for so long, their precious land, in the hands of another, even of their own son. He was aware that they had moved some years back to the cottage at Balree because his grandfather was almost crippled with rheumatism. If he had not been, they would still have been at Achnagreine, the place they loved.

But in their cottage Danny was welcomed like a king. It was little but Gaelic he heard beneath the low roof of their cosy livingroom. Never simply another language to him; more a bigger world, a living link with the old, old days, a tongue that expressed exactly the feel of things, that captured the looming of a storm, or the ecstasy of a sunny morning. The words came to his own tongue as smoothly as English. And then there were the songs and stories his grandfather told him. He would have been up at Balree every day if his parents had let him; after all it was only two miles up the glen.

What had really taken a very long time to fathom, though, was the strange, vexed question of his grandmother's second sight. Again his mind went back over the years, and he smiled inwardly as he remembered the first time it was mentioned to him; he had been a very small boy, not long in school, when a class-mate had said to him: 'My mother says your granny has the second sight.' It had not bothered him at all - of course, his granny had just got her first pair of spectacles! That must be what they meant. Gradually, as the years went past, he learned the truth bit by bit. How little adults give credit to children, or at least to sensitive children, for their awareness, he mused. He had learned to listen, while pretending to be totally absorbed in his own pursuits, when women visiting his mother would adopt a certain tone, an air of secrecy, a sort of conspiratorial whispering. And he heard more than once of how at times his granny, walking with a friend, had moved to the side of the road to allow a funeral to go past; the friend had of course seen nothing. But his granny would have 'seen' the chief mourners and knew who was about to die. There was another time, too, when her sister was seriously ill following an operation - they had always been close to each other although Mairi had been in Canada for many a long year. It seemed that his granny had known the exact hour she had been taken ill; she had noted it, and this had been confirmed later in a letter.

These pieces of information, stealthily acquired, bothered him greatly; he would lie in bed at night turning them over in his mind. Was his granny queer in some way? And then he would go up to Balree, and there she would be in the warmth of the kitchen with the range glowing red, and the delicious smell of the oatcakes she was baking would start his mouth watering; and she would turn round with her special smile of welcome, her face flushed with the heat of the fire. And he thought how stupid he had been to worry; there was nothing queer about her at all. She was the kindest and the wisest person he knew. And anyway she was his granny and he loved her.

One day when he was perhaps about twelve, he finally dared to ask his mother about her.

'What is second sight, mother?' He enquired so suddenly that she was startled, and laid down the pan she was lifting with a loud clatter.

'It's . . . it's a kind of gift some people have,' she faltered.

A gift? He pondered this; to him a gift meant the present his parents gave him at New Year. How could this strange power be called a gift? He tried again.

'Is it a sort of . . . a sort of superstition?'

This time his mother showed no uncertainty at all. 'Certainly not,' she said with conviction. 'Get that out of your head this minute, Danny. Remember this - your granny is a devout Christian, a godly woman who cares nothing for superstition. And she didn't ask to have this gift.'

Then, perhaps to end the conversation, she told him the story of how his grandmother had come to this glen from the island of Skye.

She had arrived, in her teens, to go into service at the Lodge. It was then that she had seen the young and handsome Alan Drummond, up on the hill at Achnagreine in all weathers, coming down with his beautiful horses to the dykes that ran very nearly to the Lodge. For long enough he did not appear to see her, despite many efforts, discreet though they were, on her part. But he saw her in the end - she made sure of that.

Mrs Bolton, the laird's wife, was a tyrant towards her servants and would not have contemplated allowing any courtship while Eliza was in her service. But she had not reckoned with this girl; she was not to be deterred that easily. Every Saturday evening Mrs Bolton, dressed in her fine tweeds, set out in her carriage to visit her only close friend in the district, an elderly lady who had lived most of her life in London but who had come, nobody knew why, to live in a small lodge near Drumbeg with two servants to look after her. It gave Eliza her only chance. Hoisting her long skirts to climb the dyke at the rear of the Lodge, she would speed through the damp grass towards the lights of Achnagreine whenever the carriage was out of sight. Quiet as a moth, she would return before the lady of the house, slipping stealthily up the back stairs, afraid lest the servants too would hear her and their suspicions be aroused.

But one night the end came. Mistress Bolton set off down the glen at her usual time, only to find that the road was flooded at one point. On her early return, she had called at once for Eliza. The housekeeper could not find her and her room was empty. Furious, the old lady had summoned her to the breakfast table next morning and demanded an explanation and an apology. Neither was forthcoming; Eliza had no intention of humiliating herself before this selfish woman who had virtually imprisoned her servants within the Lodge walls. Mrs Bolton, surprised and angered by this stubborn pride, told her to leave that very day. What was Eliza to do? Alan had been slow to take the hint; it was time, she decided, to make things clear. He spotted her from the stables as she dragged her cumbersome trunk down the steps; he had come running over, tearing his cap from his head, and had seen her standing in the sunlight smiling at him.

'Eliza, you can't be going!' he cried.

'No,' she had calmly replied, 'I'm coming,' nodding in the direction of the house. And so it had been. He had taken her home to his parents, who had arranged lodgings for her with the gamekeeper's wife for a few days until their marriage could be arranged.

'I'm coming!' These were the famous words she often quoted to tease her husband, as Dan crouched on the rug in front of a roaring fire. Alan would merely grunt as he sat chewing on his old pipe, but the two would exchange a laughing glance which was full of understanding. They were a couple completely at ease with each other.

What Dan loved most of all when he was up at Balree was Granny's Old Box. It was a small battered tin trunk, filled with pieces of the past, which she would drag out from under the bed. There was a box full of gemstones, faceted stones that flashed red and blue and gold when he held them up to the light. There were marbles, made of clay that Alan himself had found at Achnagreine, and soldiers made of tin which could join battle on the kitchen floor - they were Redcoats, hunting Jacobites in the hills, and they always lost. There were his granny's wedding gloves, silvery grey with a fine sheen on them, and mother-of-pearl buttons. And there were drawings, childish drawings quite unlike his mother's expert ones, tattered at the edges now, but still vivid with the wide sea and the distant Cuillins, in Elgol on the Isle of Skye where her childhood has been spent. Danny had never seen the sea, yet felt himself at one with that world, and dreamed of going out in a fishing boat like the one in the picture, with the gulls wheeling around it.

Looking back over the long years, Dan could see how he had gradually grown very close to his grandmother, and how his mother's love and hers had meant security to him; more, it had compensated for his growing alienation from his father. His grandfather, although a kindly and cheerful figure, seemed somehow to have been always in the background; he sat by the fire smoking his pipe, coming to life only when he taught the boy the old songs, and told tales of bygone years. But he never had half the vitality of his granny. He grew to realise that she had loved his dead brother Andrew, loved him very much, and as he began to grow up, she spoke more to Dan about him.

Andrew and his father, she said, were as wary of each other as two strange collies; she did not understand why Johnny, her son, had set up barriers between them; indeed she did not always understand her son at all. Dan came to be aware that a certain incident seemed to hold the key. Once, his granny told him, when Andrew was about twelve he had been coming back from Beinn Dobhran after a day's fishing on the hill lochs; he was in a hurry, for dusk was coming on and his supper would be ready. Suddenly, in the pine wood, he heard a terrible screaming; it could almost have been a child, with its high-pitched urgency, but Andrew knew what it was. He followed the sound, his heart pounding, struggling through the deep heather until he reached the trap, one of his father's, to find the rabbit there with its forepaw caught and bleeding. Working with trembling hands, he freed the terrified creature. He could never bear to see an animal's suffering, his grandmother explained; it pained him almost more than that of a fellow human being. It was so till the end, she added, when he wrote passionately from France of the horse he had seen drowning in

21

the mud. But that night among the trees, he had told her, he felt that for once he had done something worthwhile; it was this enmity between farmers and the creatures of the wild that caused him deep distress, that in fact had made him in some ways actually hate the life at Achnagreine, so that he already knew his future could not lie there. He went on towards his home with a feeling that something had been, in a sense, restored; he was at peace with himself. But when he entered the farm kitchen, his father rose up black from the fireside; he was hauled upstairs and belted without mercy. His grief, his granny said, was far less for his own pain than for the depth of the misunderstanding between his father and himself. As she told Danny the story, he looked at her and saw tears in her eyes.

'Many a time I have prayed to be able to forgive my son,' she added quietly, 'but I have never truly forgiven him.'

One thing she never did tell him, he recalled, was that she herself had known the exact moment when Andrew had been killed in France. But his mother had told him.

Now, as an old man, Dan marvelled that the thought of what came next should still have the power to cast such a deep shadow over him. And yet, how could anyone possibly forget a thing so terrible? It was his grandfather who had told him, one day when he was up at Balree, that his granny was deeply upset because of 'a thing she had seen'. She was in bed upstairs that day; Dan had been up to take her a cup of tea, for she was recovering from a bout of sickness. He had never known her to be so quiet before; she looked at him without a smile, all the sparkle completely gone out of her. He did not know what to say himself, so sat silently with his arm around her shoulders while she drank the tea. Then she simply said: 'You're a good lad, Danny,' and lay down with a long sigh; and he tiptoed away, a dark cloud on his spirit.

'Aye, she's in a bad way,' was all his grandfather said, which worried him even more. He was about to leave when his grandfather asked him to tell his father to come up that evening - another thing so extremely unusual as to cause him concern again. When he arrived home and passed on the message his father only grunted.

He was a long time in sleeping that night. The weather was hot and sultry and he tossed and turned, finally falling into an uneasy sleep. Some hours later, he awoke to the sound of voices from the next room. He knew at once that his father and mother were having an argument. Very quietly he got up and, trembling lest he should be discovered, crouched by their door and listened. At first he could make out nothing; then his father's voice was raised in anger:

'For the last time I'm telling you, Rena, I will not go and make a fool of myself telling them a foolish old woman's fancies.'

There was a pause, and he heard his mother reply, but could not hear what she said. Again his father's voice, with an edge to it:

'I'm telling you, woman, I will not do it! They'll say it's just superstition, and they'll be right.'

Afterwards he was sure he heard his mother crying, but did not dare to intrude. He went miserably back to bed, and eventually slept.

It was August, and the school holidays; he got up later than usual and found that his father was out attending to the animals. His mother looked drained, as if she had not slept a wink. He burst out at once:

'I know my granny has seen something terrible - tell me what it is.'

His mother hesitated for a moment, then answered quietly 'She says she has seen the Lodge burned to the ground and some of the family lost. She . . . she begged your father to warn them, but he refuses to do it.'

Dan was speechless, horrified; it was even worse than he had imagined. Just then his father came in. His mother brought the porridge to the table; his father said grace and they ate, then he pushed back his chair and went out, with no word spoken. Dan watched him and saw that he was deeply upset. He now saw him go with Corrie into the high field, where he set about mending a fence. Still Dan kept watching him; he hung about the kitchen with no will to do anything, until his mother sent him out to cut kindling for the fire; stifling hot though the day was, cooking still had to be done on the kitchen range.

When he returned with the wood, he could not help asking his mother what she felt about his grandmother's fears.

'I don't honestly know, Danny,' she replied with a sigh. 'All we can do is pray that she's wrong . . . this time'.

But he knew that she would be, like himself, thinking of the many times she had not been wrong. He looked at his mother with love - her long delicate hands, far too delicate, he thought, for some of the rough work she had to do; soft hair tied back so that it left her white forehead bare. The sun fell in a dusty pillar from the window, flickering and golden. His gaze then turned back to the far, bent form of his father, the hammer swinging in a wide arc as he drove a new post into the hard earth.

Dan hated these August days when the sun turned the sky copper and there was not a breath of wind, the hills shrouded in a pale haze of heat. Only hives of midges danced over the yard, weaving their grey patterns and then shifting without warning into new circles. He felt within himself a mixture of fear and excitement; he did not want to feel excited, and felt guilty about it, but he was, and that was the truth. Yet a battle went on in his spirit. Why did his father not warn the Boltons? How could he go on working up there in the field, with this terrible thing hanging over them all? In a way he under- stood, though. They probably would laugh, and call the whole thing superstition. They would not know what Highland folk had known for centuries. His father would be ashamed; and anyway, his strong religious beliefs ob- viously made him deeply uneasy over this strange gift his mother had. But she shared these beliefs, Dan thought; as his mother had once told him, she had not asked for this gift. It was all too much for him.

He thought again about the Bolton family. Granny Drummond had told him plenty of stories, from her days in service in the Lodge, about old Rachel Bolton and her selfish and cruel ways. But since then a generation had gone by. Rachel had died a sad, wandered old woman, and since she had no children her nephew, a business man in London, had fallen heir to the estate. He had come north for the shooting once or twice, but had little inclination for the dreary autumns in the glen, nor indeed for the house and gardens which were slowly falling into disrepair. He would have sold up without a second thought had it not been for his wife. Cornelia Bolton had become almost obsessively loyal to the family since she had married Roger. She was aghast that he should even think of selling the estate; she saw it as a symbol of their past which they could not lightly cast off, an inheritance Rachel Bolton had intended them to preserve. Besides, it would be good for their young son Charles to spend his summers in the glen, rather than in London. And she and Roger could hold parties there, become acquainted with the country gentry and invite friends north for the shooting and fishing. Eventually her husband reluctantly agreed, not without some misgivings that it would be throwing good money after bad.

So the Lodge came to life again, with its summer staff and the family from London. Roger, after spending the first two seasons pottering rather aimlessly in the garden and working on business reports, began to take an interest in the place, and found enjoyment in taking his son to fish the hill lochs. On one occasion Johnny Drummond had been approached and asked politely whether his son Andrew would be willing to teach young Charles the finer points of fly-fishing; curtly he replied that he was too busy. It was customary for the Boltons to hold open house on their last evening before returning south, as a gesture of friendship to the glen folk; no invitation came that year to the Drummonds of Achnagreine. Johnny merely snorted; he would be happy, he said, never to set foot in the Lodge again in his life, after all he had heard from his mother of her unhappy days there. But they all knew the enmity went far deeper than that. Once, before Johnny was born, Rachel Bolton had threatened to turn his father off Achnagreine, asserting that she could do so whenever she chose; the fear of this had remained with his father until he left the farm for Balree - and he had passed it on to his son. Johnny, who loved Achnagreine above all else, inherited as it were a loaded gun of pride and defensiveness which was forever pointed towards the Lodge.

So it was that, on a thundery day in August with the threat of something terrible hanging over them all, Danny, aware at least to some extent of the struggle which must be going on in his father's mind, could not settle to any of his usual tasks, and told his mother he was going up the river to Donnie's Pool to have a swim. He found the pool too shallow now for swimming, but he sunned himself on a rock and watched a pair of buzzards circling high above, as though caught in their own blue whirlpool. Still he felt listless and heavy, ill at ease. The sky was beginning to cloud over, seeming to be laced on every side with yellow-orange flames that melted and swelled; the heat was oppressive; not a breath moved the branches of the low birches around the river.

Suddenly he thought of his grandmother. She had been ill, and he had not even been back to see her; he knew that it was concern for her that was partly possessing him. He would go at once to Balree! In a few leaps he was back on the Achnagreine side of the burn; if he followed the same way back, it would be gentler going with the sheep track most of the way; but there was always the chance that his mother would want him and he would be kept at home. If he traversed the slopes above the house, he could come down to the road from above the Lodge and save himself a good deal of extra walking. But it would be tiring crossing the steep slope with its heather and bracken. All the same, he would go that way, he decided. He soon caught a glimpse of his father, a tiny figure in the yard, working as always in his long sleeves despite the heat.

Half way over, he flung himself in the heather, hot and panting. For a moment he was tempted to go down the hill and home; there was still a long way between him and Balree, and a good deal of it uphill. But he was worried about his grandmother, so he got up and went on. Down in the Lodge garden, he could see a little circle of deck-chairs; garish and out of place they seemed to him with the moors about them. There will be visitors up from London, he said to himself. Perhaps Charles has come on holiday. And then, despite the brassy heat of the day, a chill darkness seemed to come about him like a cloak. I am imagining things, he told himself; I have become obsessed by this whole business. Surely my granny must have been wrong; after all, time has passed. So he willed himself not to look at the Lodge again, and continued across until he came to the steep brae with its birch wood; and the road came in sight, curling on its way to Balree. It was good to come into the shade of the trees, and he found a small burn that still had a trickle of water in it, and he drank, and rubbed some water thankfully on his face.

Going into the cottage, he felt the still cool of the kitchen. No fire burned in the grate. Apprehension filled him as he went up to his granny's room. It was the old man's face he saw first, looking up pale and haggard from the chair where he sat beside his wife. Danny knelt by the bed. His granny looked fevered, ill; more, she had an unnatural quietness, a complete absence of her normal vitality which had so worried him before. Not knowing what to do, he went downstairs to fetch them both a cup of milk; then, feeling there was nothing more he could do, he left for home. He would send his mother up to look after them, he thought uneasily. He began to run as fast as he could, hardly knowing why; suddenly he felt he simply must make his father understand that this terrible thing was making his granny suffer too much. It was far more serious than a mere feverish illness. He began to rehearse what he would say to his father; for once, he decided, he really would stand up to him, challenge him.

And then suddenly, in the stillness of the coming dusk, he saw a tiny fork of lightning stab the earth. Scared now, he ran faster than ever; he went so fast that he could feel the breeze on his face. But then, almost home, he rounded the corner and stood stock still in sheer unbelief. In the midst of the trees, above the road and through the thick banks of rhododendrons, he saw the red anger of flames. There was a smell in the air, thick and heavy, like that of an October bonfire - a smell he would never be able to forget. The Lodge was burning.

The elderly couple, Cornelia and Roger Bolton, did not retreat in time from their burning wing. He had been out in the garden when Danny had passed above on his way to Balree; she had been giving the cook last-minute instructions for dinner for the first guests for the grouse shooting. She had then gone upstairs for a rest; Roger had had a drink with Charles, who had then gone to meet the guests, and had later gone upstairs himself. When the fire started, only they and the cook, with one kitchen maid, had been in the Lodge. Those downstairs had escaped easily enough; but the staircase was a mass of flames and nobody could get near.

Johnny Drummond was bringing a pail of water in from the spring when a spark caught the edge of his eye. He stood in complete horror and unbelief as they all saw the great house they knew so well rise in a tangled rose of fire, the huge flames like many adders writhing their way up into the sky. Then he ran without a word. Rena, his wife, hugged Dan to her, leaning his head against her; he wished she would stop, as two girls from the Lodge were standing near. When at last he saw his father returning, he felt he was ready at last to hurl at him all the words he had been storing up inside him for days. But when he looked at his father's face, every one of them was washed away; he looked drained, beaten. His head was bowed as if in despair; he held his big veined hands out in a gesture of hopelessness. Dan said not a word. Instead a dam seemed to burst inside him and he turned into the shelter of his mother's side and wept, as the thunder crashed far away and huge drops of boiling rain hissed against the burning ruins of the Lodge.

Chapter 4

The old man left the barn and started down the track on his way to the river. He shivered as the sharp wind caught him, the damp, cold air a man here loved and hated. There was a figure coming up towards him; he screwed up his eyes so as to see better, but it was only when he had come close that he saw it was young Roddy, Kate's son.

'How are you, Mr Drummond?' the boy said politely, his voice still a piping treble. His straw hair was tousled with the wind; Dan ruffled it kindly and stopped. He had been walking faster than usual and his breathing was not good. He smiled but did not speak. He had noticed the lilt the boy now had in his voice; although Kate was English and they had not been in the glen all that long, he was already picking up the accent. How would he ever survive at school, wondered the old man, looking with sympathy at the pale city face and the arms thin as a sparrow's; the farmers' lads could tear him apart if they chose. He seemed a lonely fellow too, Roddy; he almost gave the impression of preferring animals to folk, and had no desire to learn to fish, or even to explore the magical woods Dan had so loved as a boy.

'On you go up to the house,' Dan said to him now, 'I'm sure your mother will have the kettle on.'

'I'll not go in,' answered the boy doubtfully; and then, brightening, 'Has Charlie had her kittens yet?'

It was Kate who had given the cat its name; Dan would never have bothered. The original name, Charlotte, had rung oddly in their ears and had been pared down to the Jacobite 'Charlie'. Dan was not sure about the kittens. Kate had said nothing to him, and he realised he hadn't seen the cat for days. But he guessed that all was not well between Roddy and his mother. She seemed at times to find him a nuisance, and preferred not to have him round her feet when she was at Achnagreine helping Dan. That meant the boy was often alone in the cottage down at Shian. Kate had come to the glen with no husband, and Roddy had never spoken of a father; Dan had never liked to enquire. He wished he could have spent time with the lonely youngster, perhaps taken him to places this spring where there would be wren's nests, or to the stones under the old bridge where the otters had always had their road and where their fishbones were to be found. But he could be sure of nothing. He no longer knew how he would feel from one day to the next; he was weak now after the long, hard winter; some days he had hardly gone out at all, indeed at times he had done no more than cross the yard from the house from one week's beginning to its end. Now the wind caught him again, making him shiver; he had been going to say he might take him to Donnie's Pool, but the words never came. He turned away; it was too late now.

He came down towards the ford. The thaw had set in; the bushes hung black and dead. He felt they were like himself; the landscape and he had in a sense become one. As far as his eyes could see on every side, this was his world; this was himself. Here were his ghosts. The hands of his grandmother in the twigs of the alder; his father in the never-ending fall and toil of the burn; his mother Beinn Dobhran itself, watching and guarding, blessing with the unchanging strength of her love. He was becoming fanciful, he knew; but these thoughts comforted him. What indeed had he ever known besides? His brother's death, two wars, the loss of Catriona. Now he was here alone, but the land at least remained. The land, his own land! How could anyone fully understand what it meant to him? He remembered his father, how he would say it was idolatry to love the land too much; it was the Creator, not what had been created, that one must be sure to worship. He should have heeded his own words, Dan thought wryly: had he not also loved the land too much?

Now Dan bent down painfully towards the burn and, hardly knowing what he did, plunged his hands into its freezing water, burying them in the deep silt. The burn, he thought to himself, did not change; it did not alter for a moment its endless rushing, but went on and on until its end. Just so, nothing he himself did would alter even one iota the course of time; nobody would see his footprints any more than they would see the marks of his hands where they had been in the wild surge of the stream. Was that then what he was afraid of? That he would pass without notice? That the people would go by in their cars and never know he had been here at all? That the field would cover him with its own blanket of grass, and nobody even remember?

He went over the burn, turned and looked back at the house, with its jagged pencil of brown smoke etched against the low grey skies. And immediately there returned to his mind a vivid memory of another day, a day he would always remember. Even now, as clear as could be, he saw the figure of his father on the other side of the burn, could hear him calling - he had had to go nearer in order to hear, with the noise of the autumn spate loud in his ears:

'The rowan tree! The old tree behind the barn - it's going to have to come down! Its roots are cracking the barn floor. Don't be long coming back, I need your help!'

He would have been about thirteen at the time, Dan thought; he was on his way to the woods, the place where he always went - for solace, or sometimes just to be alone and think his own thoughts. It seemed to him that he found there something new every time he went. And, give his father his due, he never tried to stop him, provided all the jobs around the house and steading were done. Now, in answer to his father's shout for assistance, he did not shout back but merely nodded; it was little enough his father ever talked to him, except about work that needed doing about the place.

Looking back now over the long years, Dan still wondered what had been eating at his father; why was it that he had grown away from his mother and himself, seeming to withdraw into some far place deep inside himself, to be always searching, never at ease? Even on the

Sabbath, which used to be his delight - when he made sure Rena had put flowers in the parlour, and kept a good fire going in that fusty room - even on that day he would go often to the window, his eyes searching out the fields like those of a merlin, restless, withdrawn. Dan would watch him, see the light striking the deep ditches that were coming into his forehead, and the dark hair becoming streaked with grey. Was that it, the boy used to wonder, was his father afraid of growing old? And then there was the land - the love of it, but at the same time the desire somehow to tame it. The young Dan had struggled to understand, dimly aware of some kind of battle his father was fighting within. His mother never complained, never talked of any of it, but the strain showed in her face; and she and Dan drew closer together for comfort. Dan would watch her as she sat quietly sewing, and wonder at her patience and calm.

On the day the rowan was cut down, he remembered, he had gone up to the edge of the wood and sat on the barrow, that strange hillock which long, long ago had been raised for a burial mound - a place of rest, he thought, for the very first men to come to this land, the ones who hunted animals and cut down trees. Again and again he would go there, seeming to feel in it some kind of peace; he would feel part of the earth, and not detached and alone.

He left the barrow and went into the wood. He loved to listen to the wind among these autumn boughs; the beech leaves were curled and dry now and made a hissing sound. He went silently, as he had learned to do long since, hoping for the sight of a squirrel, perhaps, or the white rump of a roe deer. Sometimes he would choose a certain place where the course of the burn became a bottle-neck and, finding a supply of moss and silt, would work feverishly for a while constructing a dam. From time to time he would bring one or two chosen friends there, but he liked best to be alone; it was his place which held so much of what he most loved.

He thought of the wood as a haven, and of the barrow as its guard. Sometimes when the gamekeeper from the Lodge appeared from the western edge of the wood, he would drop down and lie flat and absolutely still until he had passed. How he resented that intrusion into his private, precious world! This was his place; nobody must spoil it or take it away from him.

He remembered that his father had asked him to return early - but realised that he did not want to go back, did not want to help his father cut down the old rowan. He loved that tree; he felt it was like being asked to assist in a murder. The previous spring a blackbird had built its nest in the branches; Dan clearly recalled how the three of them had laughed as they watched from the kitchen window the young fledglings, huddled up on one of the branches on a cold morning, looking for all the world like bad-tempered children who could not face getting up. He thought too of the many times he had used the berries as ammunition when he was younger; he even grudged the birds their share! And his mother, with her pots of clear rowan and apple jelly - she would surely miss the tree as well.

With these thoughts going round in his head he wended his way reluctantly down towards the house. A fox was barking somewhere up on the shoulder of Beinn Dobhran. Dusk was coming earlier, he noted; there was a distinct feel of approaching winter in the air. Then he had reached the barn. His father was standing with a saw in his hand, and clean white chips of the rowan trunk were strewn around his feet. A pile of logs was stacked nearby, and there seemed to be bright red berries everywhere. His father went on sawing while Dan silently and with a heavy heart joined in the work. Then, without looking up, his father said:

'You're late.'

'Sorry,' he replied. 'I was just up in the wood. Is mother in?'

'No, she went up to Balree. Plenty of work to do here before supper.' That was all; and the sawing went on.

She went up to Balree, his father had said. That must mean his granny was poorly again, thought Dan, and a now-familiar feeling of guilt came over him. He hardly ever went to see her now. Ever since the burning of the Lodge and the death of the Boltons, his grandmother had changed. Oh, he knew they said she had never fully recovered from the strange sickness which had laid her low at that time. But it went far deeper than that. Sometimes Dan had the feeling that she actually blamed herself in some way for the tragedy - not simply that nobody had warned them, but that it was her fault. She had lost her bright spirit, the vitality that had so drawn him as a young boy to her. He could almost feel afraid of her at times because of her far-away look. And she had taken to spending more and more time in bed. Her Bible was always by the bedside; sometimes she would be reading it, but she would always lay it down when he came in, and ask him about himself; but somehow he could not share his thoughts with her as he used to do. Was it just that he was growing up, he wondered; the Old Box with its treasures no longer held the same appeal for him. But no, it was much more than that. He had in a sense lost his grandmother; she was no longer what she had been to him.

His father seldom went to Balree nowadays. Dan was fully aware that the tragedy at the Lodge, and the forewarning, had greatly frightened him as well as making him feel a deep sense of personal guilt. Perhaps, he thought, his father was actually afraid of his grandmother, or of the strange gift that she had. Dan himself had grown to hate it. Why could she not have been a normal person like other people's grandmothers? At one time he had persuaded himself that she was! His grandfather, too, was failing; he no longer sang the old Gaelic songs, nor told tales from the past. It was, Dan felt, as if he had depended on his wife for his own vitality, and now that it was gone he too was empty. He was almost bent double now with rheumatism.

So his thoughts ran as together, in silence, they toiled at the cross-cut, and the pile of logs grew. Suddenly Dan looked up at the sound of running footsteps. In the fading light he saw his mother, her skirts lifted, running towards them. His father straightened and turned.

'Granny Drummond . . . she's dead!'

Chapter 5

That night Dan cried as he had never cried before. He cried for what he remembered - the times he had run to Balree, longing to be with her and hear the Gaelic songs, seeing her busy and happy as she baked her oatcakes, telling her everything that had happened to him, and to have her go here and there with him, chattering and laughing. And then he cried for the times when he had gone up there and found another woman, her eyes without any light in them; he cried too for the times when he had not gone, had neglected her because she had changed; and guilt bled in him as he thought of his failure in love.

That autumn night he cried, hearing the wind hurling itself about the walls and roof. There would be chestnuts down at the manse, he thought, and cried again because never again would he take unopened burrs up to the cottage, to the old woman with the young heart who had loved the joy of splitting them and finding the polished treasures inside. He cried until his chest ached. He stood by the window, his curtains not yet drawn, looking up in the blue-black dark at the vague shoulder of Beinn Dobhran. Why had God taken her away from him? He knew that he was crying too so that his father would hear him; his mother had stayed up at Balree to be with the old man. He had not said a word as they ate their supper, nor afterwards as they had sat by the fire hearing the wind rising outside. He did not care; surely he could not care! His father loved only the land. He showed more kindness to his sheep, his dogs. Let him hear him crying now and know at least that he, Dan, had loved her! But there came a time when he could cry no more. He stood there still at the window, shivering with cold, too tired now to do anything but stare out at the empty whiteness of the yard as the moon broke clear through the sea of cloud and seemed to breathe over the land.

When he saw the shadow that had fallen across the floor he turned sharply, scared, and recognised the tall figure of his father. He heard his own whisper:

'I'll go to bed . . . I . . . wasn't doing anything.' At once he felt his face crumpling and the tears beginning. He staggered, as he felt the big hand on his shoulder.

'Stay there if you want, son. I never came to tell you off, but I . . . heard you . . . just wanted to see how you were.' He spoke quietly.

Dan listened, his head hung. Was this, could this be the same man? Gentle as a lamb with him, his voice as soft as his mother's might have been. But this was his father!

'Come on, back to bed, Danny, you'll catch your death by the window. Here, I'll tuck you in; lie down, that's it now. Man, your hands are cold.'

He struck a match and lit the tiny paraffin lamp by the bed, and then knelt there beside him. Dan looked at the jutting head with its swept-back greying hair, the face that looked as if it had been chipped out of granite.

'Here I am, talking to you at last,' his father went on in the same quiet voice. 'Well, Danny, maybe it had to take a thing like this. Oh, I know fine what you must be thinking; I know you're probably hating me for the sake of your granny, and I don't blame you. I'm just no good at all at showing things . . . never was, I'm afraid.' There was a moment's silence. Then: 'You know, my father was a very hard man; you never saw him like that - he was old, and he had mellowed, before you ever knew him. But he was hard on me all right, even harder than I've been on you. I don't know if I ever really loved him. But your granny! Don't ever think I didn't love *her*. When I was wee, and she could spare the time, we would do all the things you and she did together - we found nests, we gathered hazel nuts, we had picnics and boiled a kettle down by the burn. They were good times . . . but then, that was before she started . . . seeing things. After that I sort of grew away from her. The last few years . . . I couldn't bear it, Dan. I saw her getting old; I saw a kind of darkness in her; I was almost afraid of her. Afraid that her strange gift was not . . . was not of God. I found it hard to reconcile with her faith . . . and my own. Just don't ever think, though, that I didn't love her - my heart nearly broke with love!'

There was a silence, and then:

'At first I tried to tell myself she was just imagining things, it was all coincidence. But that was before . . . before the fire. After that, I found it hard to go near Balree. She had become so strange, so . . . sort-of far away'. He was quiet again for a few moments. Dan said nothing. Then his father said in a muffled voice: 'The sense of guilt - it's a terrible thing. Do you see, Dan, can you understand?'

Dan was struggling with his own thoughts. He had not dreamed ever to see this. To see white stars in his father's eyes, to hear him pleading like this; it was like some strange dream. He simply did not know how to respond.

He whispered: 'I know, father. I deserted her as well.'

Johnny looked up at that, and went on: 'I wanted to remember her the way she used to be. Out in the field, I would remember a thousand things . . . there's just so much to be sorry for . . . all I said; all I did . . . Andrew especially. Nothing of it can be changed - nothing. It's too late.'

In the dim light, his face seemed to Dan like a twisted mask. He was not sure that he fully understood. But that he had come, that he was here by his side and had said he loved his granny, that was enough! Dan pulled the blankets round him and nestled his head on the pillow, and nodded gently. His father straightened slowly and stood by the bedside, as if unwilling to leave.

'Pray for me, Dan', he said. 'Maybe you think I'm a strong man. I'm not. I need your prayers'. Again Dan nodded, finding no words.

Then he said 'Father, can I come to the funeral?'

'Aye, lad, You can come.' Johnny turned and left the room.

That day of rain - he would never forget. The cottage at Balree, with the people crowded into the tiny parlour - the church was never used for funerals in those days - the smell of damp clothes; his grandfather, a man who had been tall, stooped and broken now, holding the book of psalms close to his eyes; his father, gone back as though to stone, his face without expression. His mother, beautiful under all the weight of her black, slipping her cold hand into his for comfort. And the coffin standing there; was his grandmother really inside it? Would he really never see her again, never have the chance to tell her he was sorry for neglecting her? He had not even said good-bye, he thought. He had no tears left now, and felt no desire to cry; he just felt something precious had gone from his life.

The old minister was there, standing inside the front door so that the many crowded outside in the rain could hear, speaking of Mrs Drummond's strong faith and Christian love; and as they sang, in Gaelic, the 23rd psalm the tide broke over him again and the tears came to choke him. Strangely, it was of the rowan tree that he thought at that moment - the tree which had borne such beautiful fruit and now was gone. And his granny too, had gone forever. The singing, with its poignant cadences, died away; there was a final prayer, and then the coffin was lifted by strong men, and the procession began to move away. Dan could not help at that moment feeling proud that he was one of the men; women and children never went to the graveside, but today he was to go. They had tramped in silence to the ancient burial-ground, and had stood quietly by the open grave; then his father, his face deathly pale against the black suit, stepped over and bent to whisper:

'The minister says you are to hold one of the cords.'

But Dan had turned away, shaking his head, unable to speak. His father had not insisted. He had stood a few feet away then, hearing the dull thud of the clods of earth drumming down on the shiny wood of the box. It seemed to go on and on, until he wanted to scream for them to

40

stop. He felt desperate to shut out the noise and run away from them all, out of the graveyard and up to Balree. And then it came to him that there would be nothing left there - no kettle on the boil, no Gaelic songs, no smell of oatcakes baking. It had not struck him until that moment; he had not imagined the gaping hole that would be left. In the distance he heard the river pounding, following its course through the glen, down to Abercree and, in the end, to the sea. His father was suddenly by his side, was holding his shoulders as if to stay his crying. Then it was over. The men moved away in fragmented groups. Most of the glen people had been there to bid farewell to Eliza Drummond, who had come as a girl from the Islands, but had become one of them.

Johnny Drummond had walked with his father, Alan, out through the iron gate. The minister had shaken hands with them silently and left. Dan had followed, seeing how slowly his grandfather walked, his head bent, his eyes on the deep gravel of the path. At first nobody spoke; then:

'You'll come to stay with us now, father,' Johnny said quietly; it was a statement rather than a question, and no answer was either required or received. Indeed, the old man had not spoken a word all day that Dan had heard; he had looked closely at his grandfather, and although he seemed to have aged already and his face was haggard and pale, yet there seemed almost to be an air of serenity about him. Did he perhaps feel it would not be long till he and she were reunited, the boy wondered. Now his father told him to go on ahead to Achnagreine so that his mother could have a meal ready; he left them in their painfully slow walk, and ran as quickly as he could. His mother held him in a warm embrace when he arrived, but they said little.

At last the two men arrived. Rena had a blazing fire going in the range; the room was bright and welcoming. They sat down at the table and the old man, as the senior, said grace before the meal.

Later, Dan and his grandfather sat at the fire while Johnny made ready to go back up to Balree for those things which would be needed for the time being. Dan felt awkward with his grandfather, so unused was he to seeing him sitting there, and he searched his mind for something to say. Then his father came in bearing an armful of logs.

'They're not really ready for burning yet,' he said to his wife, 'but seeing the fire's so hot, they'll keep it going for a good while.' Then he went out.

Old Alan sat looking at the fire for a moment then, for the first time apart from asking the blessing, he spoke.

'Rowan logs?' he said to Rena. 'He didn't . . . didn't cut down the old rowan?'

Dan's mother nodded gently.

'The rowan.' He was almost whimpering now. 'It's been there as long as I can remember . . . what possessed him? She would never have let him, never!' Gently then, Rena led him up to his room.

Chapter 6

Dan stood still on the far side of the burn. Roddy, Kate's boy, had disappeared. The old man was alone there, his eyes half-mesmerised by the silver flow of the water as it gushed down dark among the pools like a great serpent. Through a small break in the clouds the sun spread out in sudden gold over the land; but down the glen towards Abercree a great grey wall had fallen. The lambing snow! That would be it; the snow his father had so feared, and his grandfather before him. How often Dan had known it; he recalled how the newborn scraps had lain crumpled and shivering beside the ewes, hardly able to bleat for weakness and cold. The snow, he thought, was a more dangerous enemy than any eagle or fox, and no bullet in the world could defeat it. For all the changes he had seen - the new machinery, the sprays and fertilisers - the enemies had not gone. He did not truly think of the animals as enemies; after all, this was their land too - the fox and the badger, the otter and the roe deer, that sometimes raided his crops.

But once he had lost three lambs in the space of one weekend; the carcasses had been left half-eaten in the top field, below the first scree slopes of the Beinn. It had been a hard winter that year; deer, pathetic in their straggling groups, had come low down in their desperate search for food. That time he knew the killings had been the work of a fox, and a hungry one at that. And on the Sabbath he had waited, watching the crystals of snow drop against the light of the lamp. At dawn the snow had stopped, the skies breaking with blue as delicate as a hedge sparrow's egg. He took his gun, and began the steady walk up towards the woods.

He found the tracks quickly enough, here and there around the boulders strewn over the open hillsides, several sets, still quite fresh. Then, quite far away, he spotted them, a flutter of sandy red on the snows. Using whatever cover he could find, he cautiously moved higher; before very long he was near enough to shoot, and he raised the gun to his shoulder. At that moment he made a careless movement with his foot and a stone rolled noisily away. At once the mother fox turned towards him, her three cubs moving restlessly behind her. She did not move an inch, but looked steadily at him. His hand trembled; slowly he lowered the gun. Even as he did so, he could almost hear his father - and his grandfather: - 'Call yourself a man of the land? Are you out of your mind?' But what right had he? The cubs would have starved! He had killed foxes before when he had to; he would no doubt kill them again. But not this time.

His mind returned to that time after the death of Eliza, his grandmother, when her husband Alan came to stay again at Achnagreine. At first, Dan recalled, he had been silent, almost as if in a kind of daze, hardly able to take in the enormity of what had happened to him. At times, though, he would be overcome with grief. Crippled as he was, he could do little apart from sitting at the fire; Dan remembered how his mother, with her customary kindness, invariably saw to it that a cheerful blaze was kept going in the kitchen range at all hours. Never again did old Alan refer to the rowan tree.

Dan could not help but notice with what respect Johnny treated his father. In the matter of family worship, for example; as the senior, he was the one to read aloud from the Bible; he it was who also asked a blessing on their meals together.

It seemed now to Dan, looking back, that after a while - he could not be sure just how long - old Alan settled down with the three of them with a surprising serenity; indeed, he remembered it as a happy time in many ways. Thinking of it now, what came back to him was the life of the glen in all its fullness - the ordinary days, filled with hard work; the Sabbath days, when everything was different, even the dishes his mother would bring out, and the best tablecloth and few pieces of silver; visits from neighbours, when there would be much talk and laughter around the fire. You never invited folk in those days, thought Dan - they called at any hour, and the kettle was never far off the boil. And there were the special occasions, of which New Year was the chief (Christmas was an ordinary working day then); but sometimes, for no particular reason, the parlour fire would be on, and in would come a few of his parents' musical friends - Alasdair the roadman with his fiddle, young Iain from the next farm with the old 'squeeze-box' his uncle had sent him, and on which he performed with amazing skill; Peter the post with his 'trump', as they called the Jew's harp. What great nights they were, thought Dan wistfully; when he was very young he would be sent to bed far too early for his liking, and he would creep out of bed and stand outside his bedroom door to hear the music, caring nothing for his icy feet. Sometimes his mother would sing in her lovely, slightly husky voice; it was always a Gaelic song, and it was always a sad one because, she said, they were the most beautiful; and always Dan would have a lump in his throat, and would feel ashamed, because tears were for girls. There was never any drink on these occasions, Dan remembered, not like nowadays; only at New Year would the whisky bottle - otherwise kept for medicinal purposes - be brought out, with glasses on a tray; for the women there would be home-made ginger wine, always served along with his mother's shortbread, dainty pieces cut in crescent and diamond shapes for the occasion.

How well he remembered the humour; there was always plenty of it in the glen, even when times were hard - maybe especially at those times. And nobody, he thought, had seemed to mind the same old jokes being told over and over, not like today, when radio and television had made folk much more demanding. Old Calum from up at Camus Lurgan, now, he was a great one for poaching stories; he had a fund of them which nobody ever tired of hearing. He was a natural story-teller; he would punctuate his tales with remarks like: 'Boys, you'll never guess what happened then!' so that you hung on

his words even although you knew fine what the out-
come had been.

Some of the glen humour was connected with the
nicknames - common, and indeed necessary, in an area
where many had the same surnames. He recalled especially Peter the miller, known as 'East-West' because of
his habit of mentioning the direction - it was always 'east
to Drumbeg' or 'west to the barn'. Whether he was aware
of his nickname or not, nobody knew - until one evening
by the fire, when the tea was being passed round; Alasdair the roadman handed him the plate of scones, saying
slyly, without even a glimmer of a smile, 'Put west your
hand and take east a scone.' There was a moment of silence, and then Peter had thrown back his head and
roared with laughter; delightedly they had all joined in.
Some of the names were more obscure, their origins long
since forgotten - like Kate the Hind, and Maggie Heather;
some merely incorporated a feature of the person concerned, like 'ruadh' for red-haired; while sometimes an
entire family of children had their father's christian name
tacked on to their own.

Humour reached a kind of climax at Hallowe'en,
though, Dan reflected. In those days, it had far more to
do with practical jokes and sheer fun and games than
nowadays, with all the talk of witches and spells. As a
child he had dressed up in a weird collection of old
clothes, topped off perhaps with a bonnet of his father's,
and with his face blackened; and he was allowed to go
'guising' to a few of the houses within easy reach, to recite a poem or sing a song, and then be recognised, or
not, by the occupants. But it was the 'big boys' who
played the pranks. One Hallowe'en, he remembered, a
gang of them had taken away all the gates in the neigh-
bourhood - they had found their own gate next day at the
bottom of a pile, neatly stacked beside the road. And then
there was the time the chimney smoked so badly that his
father had to get a ladder and climb up to find out the
reason - which was a huge turnip somebody had placed
on top. But for the children, there was not only the fun of

'dooking' for apples, but the almost unknown thrill of being given some pennies; they got nuts and apples too, but the houses at which pennies were given were noted for following years.

April Fool's Day, the first of April, was another time for practical jokes. Dan could remember some of these vividly; some of the older generation, he thought, were merciless on the youngsters in those days - sending them all the way to the shop in Drumbeg to buy a tin of elbow grease, or tartan paint. Or giving them a letter for some friend, with a note inside saying 'Don't laugh, don't smile, send the fool another mile.' Dan had himself once been the victim; it was a long time before somebody finally took pity on him.

Then Dan started to think about New Year again; it was the real highlight. One year he was given a sledge which his father had made for him, secretly, in one of the sheds. No gift in all his life, he felt sure, had ever given him more pleasure. He pictured the scene so clearly now, all these years later; he was beside himself with excitement, bouncing round the room like a dog that knows it is about to go out for a walk.

Then his father chuckled gently as he lit his pipe, and said mock-angrily, 'On you go then. Away and try it out before you drive us all daft.'

Never was there a sledge like that one. And making it had been good for his father, he reflected. It had brought them closer.

But that had always been the trouble - his father simply couldn't allow folk to come too near. Even on those musical evenings long ago, Dan recalled, his grandfather would often seem more part of things than his father. Johnny Drummond, although as a host he was welcoming enough, had a kind of silence about him, a withdrawn look. Yet over the years, how often Dan had comforted himself by remembering that night, the night of his grandmother's death, when for once his father had come close. How much it had meant to him, especially at those times when all his father had said to him amounted to no more than a dozen words in an entire day! Then he would hug to himself the words Johnny had spoken to him that night: 'Here I am, talking to you at last.'

Even if he never talks to me again in that way, he would say to himself, I will never, never forget.

But he remembered also how his father had often said that his own father, Alan, had been hard on him; to Dan, seeing the gentle old man who now lived with them, this was difficult to believe. And strangely enough, it was not until much later, when his grandfather began to lose his memory, to have periods of forgetfulness when he seemed to imagine himself back in the old days and master of Achnagreine again, that he began to understand that what his father had said was indeed true.

At times Alan would lash out suddenly at Dan's father, saying things like: 'I've always told you you're slow and clumsy! You'll never handle ewes for me again!'

Or at other times it was old Mrs Bolton he was addressing; the old fear of losing the precious land was on his mind. He would burst out with angry shouts of:

'Never, Rachel Bolton! I'll never let this land go! There's nothing you can do to take it from me and I'll fight, I tell you! This is my land, do you hear? You bought yours; but this belongs to my people, aye, as far back as you can go!'

A shadow of stark fear would cloud his face then - how that woman must have frightened him, thought Dan - and often he would begin to weep pitifully. And once or twice he had called out, 'Eliza! Come here! Come and tell her!' He would look around as if in a daze; then, seeming to come to himself, would crouch over the fire, and break into uncontrollable grief. Rena would exchange a look with her husband, he would nod gently; then they would take an arm each and help him slowly up the stairs to bed.

That was the beginning of the bad times, Dan remembered sadly; the period of calm was beginning to pass; gradually the lucid intervals became shorter, the outbursts more frequent. As always, Dan had been anxious about his mother; yet sometimes, noting how his grand-father could humiliate his father, he found an unfamiliar sense of sympathy for him; one time, marvelling at his forbearance with the old man, he could not help saying:

'How can you put up with it, father?'

Quietly, his father had replied, 'The fifth command-ment, Dan; remember? Honour thy father and thy mother.'

And as time went on, it was again his mother Dan worried about; sometimes she looked haggard and weary, and he noticed that she never sang at her work around the kitchen any more. It was she, after all, who had the old man on her hands all day long; he and his father could escape for hours at a time. Nowadays, he supposed, a social worker would have been involved and a suitable place found where he would have been cared for; no such things as homes for the elderly had existed in those days, at any rate not anywhere near the glen. Even if they had, he knew that his parents would never have accepted such a solution.

Once Dan had gone down to the kitchen very late at night for a glass of water; his bare feet made no sound, and he opened the door noiselessly, to find his mother sitting by the fire in her long white nightdress. She was crying. Dan wanted to go to her and put his arms round her; but he did not. He shrank away without a sound. He knew without asking what was wrong. It was a long time before he could get to sleep that night.

Then, an unexpected visit from a cousin of his mother's had brightened all their lives. Alec, a young man in his twenties, worked in a shipyard in Glasgow; he had been ill, and had been ordered by the doctor to spend some time in the fresh air of the country. Coming to the glen, with its ways so utterly new to him, had been like entering a new world; Dan now wondered who had been more astonished, Alec or themselves.

'What do you do for pleasure?' he asked one day. 'Don't you wish you had shops for all the things you need?'

'You don't miss what you've never had,' Rena replied evenly. 'The one thing I do envy you, I suppose, is electric light.'

It was some time before they noticed that the old man had been much more stable since Alec came; he seemed to sense that in the presence of a stranger his outbursts must be controlled. This, and the stimulation of Alec's lively talk, brought back to Dan's mother something of the old cheerfulness. Most of all, Dan remembered, Alec took an interest in her painting. He himself, although not a painter, produced very passable sketches; he was also in the habit of spending hours every Saturday at Kelvingrove Art Gallery. Dan noticed how his mother drank in all that he told her of the great art he had seen there. She said she really must make an effort to go; but Dan knew she never would.

The time came for Alec to depart. He had put on weight and there was colour in his cheeks. But 'the city is in my blood,' he had sighed, when they spoke to him of staying.

They all missed him when he went. And very soon they knew that the brief respite was over. Old Alan began to deteriorate rapidly. It was about Hallowe'en when Alec left; the time between then and New Year was hard. There was a kind of brokenness in the house, Dan thought, as he looked back over the years. His parents on edge: waiting, watching, pretending. Now, when visitors came to the house, his mother would often lead the old man gently up to his room. Nobody ever knew when he would break out either in anger or in grief. And so it was when another New Year was upon them, one none of them felt ready for. Dan watched his mother especially, seeing the strain showing in her face more than ever; as always, his father said little, but Dan was aware that he had become more helpful to his wife, doing jobs like feeding the hens, which normally fell to her lot.

On Hogmanay night, old Alan retired to bed soon after the evening meal. According to tradition, the glasses were laid out on a tray, with the whisky bottle, the ginger wine, and the plate of shortbread; as the night wore on, several of the neighbours came in, and were welcomed into the parlour. Alasdair the roadman, who normally brought his fiddle, had not done so out of deference to the old man, feeling that music would have been an intrusion; but young Iain had had no such reservations, and he soon began to play his melodeon, and Dan could hear the music long after he had gone up to his room. He lay awake for a while; then, as he had done so often in the past, he could not resist getting up and opening his door so as to hear better. There at the top of the stairs, leaning over the banisters, he saw his grandfather; tears glistened on his cheeks, and he looked as though his mind was far away, perhaps re-living New Years of long ago, hearing the voices of those who were long since gone. Dan shivered and went back to bed.

In the morning he awoke very early. Listening intently, he could hear no sound of drops from the roof on to the window ledge; that meant there was frost. The slide would be lethal by now! He had sluiced it with water last night; now, he decided, he would creep downstairs and have a good hour on it before anyone was up. He could hear his father snoring next door. Silently he dressed and tiptoed down to the kitchen; he chewed a piece of oatcake and drank some milk, then wrapped his thickest scarf around his neck and put on his warm mitts. He stepped over the two dogs and pulled open the door that was half-jammed with the frost.

As though he had fallen from the doorstep, the old man, his grandfather, lay there in the snow. His face was turned to one side; he seemed to be looking up to Beinn Dobhran, to the high slopes with their dark woods. A dusting of snow must have come since his fall, for on the back of his hand crystals glistened like diamonds. Dan bent down towards him, awed, looking closely at the face, at the wide-open eyes with their opaque, milky film. The mouth, half-open, reminded him of a trout when it has been landed from the river and is left lying on the bank; but the corners were turned upward, as though

51

with the vaguest hint of a smile. Blood had stained the snow beside his right temple where it must have struck the stones in his fall.

Where could he have been going? What had he wanted? Suddenly Dan saw, lying a little out of reach of his other hand, a single thin log. It was from the rowan tree.

Chapter 7

Dan remembered the face of Alan Drummond exactly as it had been on that New Year's morning. Now he shivered in the cold wind; he began to climb the steeper slopes, going slowly and steadily, yet feeling conscious of his laboured breathing, stopping every few minutes to regain strength. Was he, he wondered, becoming like his grandfather? Was there nothing left now for him except ghosts?

No! This was still his land; these were his fields. That was enough. That was the umbilical cord that kept him firmly anchored; he belonged here; he would keep going while he still had the strength.

And he was determined that now, today, he would not return to the farm until he had gone much higher; if he went back now, he knew that Kate would turn a look of triumph on him, as if to say 'I told you so.' He felt a sudden rush of anger. Who was she to invade his world, to assume some sort of power over him? He was well aware that she wanted the farm after he was gone; but she would not have it. The land did not know her; his ghosts did not know her, even although he had to admit she was good with the sheep; she had been well taught. But not here! Her ways were not his. And then he asked himself why it was that he was crossing and re-crossing the fields of the past, today especially? Surely it was because the memories of his own people were a part of him always, like photographs that did not fade. And the centre of the world was Achnagreine; always he had gone from there and always he had returned.

He came at last to the barrow and paused at its base. It was a long, high mound, with three straight pines on the summit. From their branches some rooks flew with raucous cries. Up here he felt the wind keenly; he put his hand up to his cheek and found it icy cold; his fingers, unprotected by the woollen mitts, were almost numb with cold. He stood and considered the ancient mound. Once there had been a tunnel there that led to the graves of men, perhaps the very first men who had possessed this land. Had they too felt the pain that came with age? Had they loved this place and known the dread of leaving, the awareness that soon they would not see again the evening skies as they turned loch blue and shone with a strange light as dusk came on? How beautiful it was! He sat down between two great rocks, and listened to the music of the wind in the pines. As a child, he recalled, he had imagined himself below the rigging of a tall ship, the three trees with their mighty sails ploughing through unknown waters. Now the sound brought a measure of peace to his troubled heart. He was a child again; the same trees still stood, and they held him, rocked him, sang to him. As he sat, more and more and more memories of the past surged through his mind.

Alan Drummond had been buried beside his wife in the old burial ground at Drumbeg. Dan did not go to the funeral, nor did either of his parents ask him to; they were aware of the nightmares which were plaguing him, strange dreams which brought back over and over the sight of that face in the snow, with blood staining its whiteness. But in the end even that passed; and with the return of spring, his favourite season - the delight at the coming of primroses and lambs, the hatching of chickens and ducklings, and nests to be found in the woods and moors - there was healing for him. The weeks went by and soon it was summer.

His father seemed buried in his own silence. Dan would come home from school bursting with energy, longing to run and kick a ball about the yard, eager to make things - from metal, from wood, from anything he thought might be thrown out. He would bounce around his father as he worked, sharing all his ideas - he and his friends were going to ride the river as far as Abercree in a canoe like the ones the Indians had made. Or he was going to make a special trap to catch the pheasants he had seen in the rough pasture at Drumbeg. Or could his

54

father show him how to build a hut? At times he would try to pull Johnny round by the shoulders because he felt he was not really listening. Always the answer seemed to be the same: 'Leave it till later.'

But there never was a later. His father was distant and dark, as he had been in those tense days when his grandmother had been bedridden, before the fire. It was as though he had shut himself away in some walled place, Dan thought, where nobody could reach him. And in a way, he could perhaps understand - had he not lost both his parents within a short space of time, and in tragic ways? It was no use, he would think in the end; I'll never be able to reach him. He then did what he had done before, even though he was older now and his shoulders growing broad; he went to his mother. She had always been his comfort, always a source of strength, full of energy and laughter. With her he would recapture the joy that seemed to have gone.

But it was not there. It was, he thought, as if he had gone running up to the shoulders of Beinn Dobhran in summer, looking for a stream he had known and loved, and found only the merest trickle remaining. Something terrible was wrong with his mother, he realised, with a sense of fear that almost choked him. She looked ill; pale and drawn, she moved about the kitchen with none of her old cheerfulness, none of the songs he used to love. He began to watch her covertly. He would come in from school, and find her sitting slouched in a chair, as if she was too tired to do anything else; no longer would she be baking, or ironing, or making up a hot mash for the hens. And when he asked her to come and see a mallard's nest he had found by the river, or to climb up to the wood because the wild hyacinths were in full bloom, she would say 'Dan, I'm just too tired,' or 'Your father has to have his supper early; he's helping up at Camus Lurgan with the clipping.'

She seemed to make almost as many excuses as Johnny himself did. Yet he knew, knew with a terrible sinking of his heart, that it was not that she did not want to go with him; she loved all these things as much as he did - indeed, had she not taught him to love them? No, it was simply that she no longer had the strength.

Why had he not noticed before? He had supposed it was the old man who had been too much for her. But it was more, much more. He saw the creamy pallor of her face; he realised that she was tired, drained, at the end of her tether. Not that she showed any less love to him; feeling his eyes on her as they sat together at the kitchen table sometimes, she would pick up his spread hand and hold it, stroking back the wild hair from his forehead with a gentle hand. In a way he thought her even more beautiful, with the grey lines now about her cheeks and her face thinner and her eyes with the dark shadows about them, like deep blue lochs.

But the silence of his father did not help her either. Sometimes it seemed to Dan that Johnny found it easier to show affection to his dogs than to his family; there had been a time when he had been hard on them, saying that dogs were for work - 'Pet them, and they'll laze at the fire all day', he had said. But now it was different. Dan had often seen him bending down, balanced on his heels, stroking the warm, thick coat of one or other of the collies, the dog's head stretched forward eagerly to receive the caress.

Increasingly aware of all that was wrong at home, dissatisfied with Achnagreine for the first time in his life, Dan took more and more to going out by himself - to the woods, to the river, anywhere at all as long as he could forget his worries even for a short time. That was when he had been about fifteen. School bored him. He would sit at his desk, leaning on one elbow, sleepily hearing the flies on the window pane, longing to be free. He did not know what he wanted - only that it was not this. There was a restlessness in him; he trailed home alone, telling his friends he could not be bothered playing football. After a cup of tea he would often retreat up to his room until supper-time. Then there would be jobs to do, like cutting sticks for the fire; as soon as these were done, he would say:

'I'm going out.'

'Where to?' his father always asked, a roughness in his voice that made Dan stiffen at once.

'Let the boy go, John,' his mother would say; almost always she took his side.

'Has he no lessons to do then?' Johnny would reply gruffly.

Once, his mother had boldly added, 'And what would you have him do? All his Saturdays, slaving away with you on the farm, and from Monday to Friday never looking up from his books. What kind of a life is that? You'd think you were never young yourself!'

Dan had slipped away at that point, his eyes smarting with tears. What was happening to them? Why could they not be happy together? Everything, everything had gone wrong since his granny had died, he decided. And, as he had done so often, he made for the solace of the wood, to sit and be quiet, and hear the soothing wind in the pines overhead.

Sometimes he would go straight up to the barrow without stopping, and lie face down in the soft moss; and he would wonder if holding a woman in his arms would feel as soft as this. Sometimes he would sit and look down at Achnagreine and the weak gold of its light, and then at the other farms dotted along the line of the glen, each with their own stars of brightness. At other times he was so filled with restlessness that he did not stop at all by the barrow, but went crashing on instead into the dark of the pines, hardly feeling the branches against his face; he even thought once 'If I have blood on my face maybe my father will at least notice me!' On and on he went, until at last he was free, standing there in the beautiful bowl of the corrie on Beinn Dobhran, milk-white and bare, reminding him as he turned of a giant's head. All that was in front of him now was a great expanse - loch after loch, round blue-black pools joined by deep trenches of burns. Knee-high heather all around; orchids in sum-

mer, curlews crying; all this was his, mile after mile without end. And he was free.

Yet it was not always here he sought refuge on those
days when he could bear the house no longer. Sometimes
he would start blindly down the field, past the ruins of
the Lodge, and on to the road down to Drumbeg. And
one night, still clear in his memory, his feet stopped outside the old churchyard, and he had considered; then
very quietly he had opened the heavy iron gate and gone
in, round to the strange lines of the gravestones with
their grey shadows. Nothing but the sound of the river in
his ears, and the bleating of sheep from the fields above
Drumbeg, and the scent of the trees after the rain. He
found his grandmother's grave, and brought from his
pocket a single orchid from the moor, its veins delicately
traced with mauve, the flower she had loved most in the
world. He knelt by the side of the stones; he tried to pray,
but no words came. He did not know if he wanted to
speak with this God who had taken her away and who
now threatened . . . but no, he would not even form his
fears about his mother into conscious thought. His eyes
filled with hot and bitter tears and he buried his head in
his arms.

When he felt the hand on his shoulder, he started up
in fear; then through his tears he saw the face of the new
young minister, John Maxwell.

'Come on, Dan, back to the manse for a bit.'

Dan said nothing as he went with him, feeling only
the wet grass against his ankles, aware of the intense
stillness of the evening, the glen seeming to wait for the
end of summer and the coming of harvest. The skies
were clearing and a pair of ducks went low overhead
with their quick wing-beat. He noticed an old man in the
doorway of one of the Drumbeg cottages, gently encouraging a little toddler who stomped on uncertain legs on
the path. As Dan and the minister passed, it turned its
head to look, lost its balance and fell in a helpless pile of
frustration. He felt, in self-pity, that he was somehow the
same; every time he got up and began to grow, it seemed

to him, he was knocked over; one blow came after another. How could there be a loving God? There could not be, he thought. He walked on in silence; the young minister leaving him to his thoughts.

As he was left alone in the study while the tea was made, Dan thought about John Maxwell. There had been plenty of talk in the glen since the old minister had died and he had arrived, only last autumn. The elders did not approve of him, he knew that; they said he did not keep his place, he was too familiar, too much like one of themselves; and in his preaching he was too soft, too ready to understand and forgive the failings of people. All Dan knew was that the dark cloud was gone that had hung over going to church every Sunday; he for one did not miss the stern old man in the pulpit.

'What do you want most in the world?'

John's question startled Dan as they sat by the fire, each with a cup of tea in his hands. He glanced at the minister's face in half-suspicion, but the man meant it, really wanted to know and would respect his reply. All that past year, he now thought, nobody had listened; his father merely told him what to do and became angry if he spoke back; his mother had become more turned in on herself, and because of her obvious weakness he had not felt able to share his thoughts with her as before. But this man was giving him his complete attention; he was looking at him with eyes full of concern and kindness. No-one had ever asked him this question before and he did not answer at once, wanting to be sure of his own mind.

'A real father,' he said suddenly, almost shocked at his own reply, looking into the fire and nervously tugging at his hair, adding 'someone who would go to all the places.' He looked up at John Maxwell: 'There's nobody left . . . my granny used to come when she was able . . . my mother too, but she doesn't any more. And my father...' his voice trailed away. 'It's not the same on your own.'

John nodded gently and kept his eyes fixed on Dan, as if waiting to hear if he had anything else to say. Then, bending down to lay his cup on the hearth, he said:

'I know how you love your land, Dan. Even though I don't belong to the glen I can see, and I understand. But you know, the greatest father you can have is Christ. He would have loved this glen as you do - the Beinn, the lochs, the fishing, all the things you love! He would be up early like yourself, to see the deer in the fields, the otters by the burn...'

Now it was *his* voice that trailed away, as he leaned forward to stretch out his hands to the blaze. Then he sat back and looked straight at Dan. The boy, seeing the warm intensity of that gaze, thought he had never felt safer or more at peace with anyone in his life.

'We all need a real father,' the young man went on. 'You may think I don't, because I'm a minister; that I'm strong, and never afraid. Believe me, Dan, I'm just as lonely as you are. All winter I was alone in this cold, dead old house; I've never felt so alone in all my life. But I couldn't go on living - and I mean that - if I didn't know God as my Father. He's really here, you know, as close as you are now! And on those long lonely nights I could feel His Presence. It made all the difference in the world.'

Again he was quiet for a few moments, while Dan struggled to take in what he was saying so earnestly.

'We all need an anchor in life,' he went on, 'when all that is bound by time is uncertain and shifting. The summer passes and the winter comes; those we love are taken away, again and again, without our understanding. But when you put your trust in Him, you can be quite sure He will direct your path - He really will, Dan, because He has promised! And you'll know Him as the Creator of the beauty of the hills and the moors and the river - all this place that means so much to you. Open your heart to Him, Dan - put your hand into His! You just have to have faith.'

Chapter 8

But he *had* turned away. He could not, would not believe in a God who would take away those he loved most. What kind of a God was that? If indeed there was a God at all, then he, Dan, was angry with him. He had not liked to share these thoughts, not even with the young minister who had an understanding heart. And at times he felt sad - felt that he had been, as it were, shown a door opening into a place of beauty and peace; but he could not go in.

Nor did he particularly want a Creator to thank for the land, for the glen he loved; it was enough that it was there in the morning, that it grew green in the summer, and the colours came in all their glory in the autumn, and in the winter it was bare and stark and still beautiful, and when snow covered everything the beauty was beyond description. Yes, these things were enough for him.

Another spring came and he was away in the hills more than ever. Dougie and Iain, the two brothers from higher up the glen who had long been his firmest friends, hardly saw him now, and he knew they felt he had shunned them. But he could not help it; he had to be alone to think, to try to work things out. It was fine to throw yourself into a hard game of football at school, but after school it was different - you had to have the quiet-ness of the wood, or the rocks down by the burn. He felt he wanted to empty his head of all that was being crammed into it; sometimes he was angry, finding his brain full of alien things, like adverbial clauses and the Latin gerundive and logarithms. What had these to do with his life here? It seemed as if he was sacrificing his life, his real life, for a lot of useless facts, things he had not asked to learn and would never need again. It was his life; why should he waste precious days on things he cared nothing about? As a result of thoughts like these, on some days now he plucked up courage not to do his homework; either that, or he would be out of the house until late at night and forget about it altogether.

'Well, Drummond, what about those geometry problems I set you?'

'I haven't done them, sir.'

Old Murray, whom they called Kaiser Bill, looked coldly at him with raised eyebrows. He got up slowly from his desk and paced slowly to Dan's seat, the immaculately polished brogues scraping on the hard floor.

'This is not good enough, boy'. His voice was ominously quiet. There was not a sound as each pupil leaned forward, waiting to see if Dan would be punished there and then. 'You'll do your work exactly when I tell you to, Drummond,' the master continued, pulling Dan roughly to his feet. 'And come and see me when we've finished for the day.'

Dan was not frightened, not any more. He simply did not care. He had had plenty of beatings from his father in the past; but Johnny Drummond did not beat him any more, not now that he was as tall as himself. Sometimes it seemed to the boy that they faced up to each other like two dogs and then retreated. So now he looked out at the fields around the school, and wondered what the Kaiser meant to do, what he would say to him. He could belt him if he liked. He did not care.

'I'm disappointed in you, Dan.' The old teacher was sitting in his chair looking up at him, and he seemed more sad than angry, Dan thought. His eyes even held a hint of a smile; and he had used his christian name. 'You want me to believe you're no good at your work; but you know, and so do I, that that's just not true. You have a good brain, boy; there's a lot more in that head of yours than fishing and shearing sheep.'

Dan had said nothing. In those far-away days, Dan mused, pupils were not expected to reply; today it was different - the pupils seemed to be on familiar terms with their teachers. He remembered clearly how he had hesitated even to ask a question about something he did not understand. On that day, he had simply sat looking out of the window, seeing his own reflection, his face thin and dark and resentful. Then he looked back and saw the old teacher's eyes still fixed upon him.

'In a year's time, Dan, there's the bursary examination for university. I want you to take it'.

To his own surprise, Dan found himself saying fiercely:

'No!'

Mr Murray's face seemed to change for a moment; a look of anger flashed, but he held himself in check, and then continued in the same quiet, even voice:

'I'm not going to argue with you now. But at least listen to what I'm saying. Don't lock yourself away. I've seen fine students in this school, with promise and fame so near their hands they could have reached out and touched them. But no - they were as stubborn as you, and they never went further than the market at Abercree, never read a book again apart from the Bible. And aye, they believed they needed nothing else; the glen was enough, year in, year out, good years and bad. But there were some that regretted it, bitterly regretted the wasted opportunities, when it was too late.'

There was a silence and then the old man got up, as if wearily. Dan saw that he looked tired, tired and old; an air of heavy sadness was all about him.

Dan asked, 'May I go now, sir?'

The teacher nodded. But as Dan turned to go, he seemed to pull himself up and in a strong voice said:

'I'll not say this again, Dan; put your mind to your work and you'll go far.'

'Thank you sir,' Dan replied, in a tone of meekness he was far from feeling. His thoughts were turbulent as he left the building. 'I'll go far, will I?' he muttered angrily to himself. 'The old fool - where does he think I want to go but here? To some horrible town, perhaps, to teach a lot of stupid children and end up old and tired and done like himself? Does he not realise I have everything, everything in the world I need, in this glen?'

Yet he did not forget the old teacher's words. And once he had calmed down, he could not help feeling proud that Kaiser Bill, one of the strictest teachers in the school, should have singled him out and spoken to him as he had.

At home he felt a deeper unease than ever. His mother was far from well; she seemed at times to drag herself around; she was deathly pale and her eyes always looked sleepless, strained. Her face was thinner, drawn, its beauty withering and yet somehow sharper, more striking.

'Go to the doctor, mother,' he said, more than once.

'I'm fine, Dan, just tired,' was her invariable reply. She would smile gently at him and he would smile back, but his whole being ached with the dread he felt; he had an overwhelming desire to guard her, protect her. And at times a kind of blind anger at his father came over him; he would look at him sitting by the fire, seemingly unaware of the terror that filled his son's heart. It was the silence that was hardest to bear, the silence that seemed to Dan to be made up of their three minds waiting, listening in the shadows of their own thoughts, wondering. Worst of all was the silence at the table as they ate, not looking at one another, keeping their heads down. Once, his mother had suddenly broken down; she dropped her knife and fork so that they fell from the table and clattered to the floor. Then she ran from the room, stifling her sobs. For a moment or two he had sat there, willing his father to go after her. Then, still half in doubt, he stood up and scraped back his chair.

'She'll be all right,' Johnny muttered with his mouth full. 'No need for you to move.'

'I'll go if I damned well want to!' he had suddenly shouted at his father; the words were out before he could stop them. As he banged the door, he heard a muffled shout from his father in reply:

'You dare to swear in this house!'

He took no notice, but knocked on his mother's door and went in. But what was there to say to her as she knelt

64

by her bed crying? He felt awkward, an intruder; the words he wanted to say would not come. As a child he could so easily pour out all the empty promises - that he loved her and would never leave her, that she always would be the closest to him. Now he longed to assure her of his love, but he could not. He still loved her with intensity; yet in some way he was also aware that the umbilical link was broken; things could never be again as they had been in childhood. Knowing her deep hurt, he felt at that moment all the more helpless. His silence was in a sense worse than his father's.

One day he came home from school and knew at once, from the remembered smell of the doctor's tobacco, that he had been there to visit his mother. His heart began to thump uncontrollably with fear; what could have happened? There was no sign of his mother or of supper. Almost at once Johnny came in; Dan knew he must ask him what was wrong, but at first he simply could not frame the words. Each time he tried, his tongue seemed to be frozen. Then the dread question was out:

'What is wrong with mother?' Johnny's back was turned; he did not answer for what seemed like an eternity. Then he turned to face Dan.

'The doctor says it's . . . it's some kind of anaemia,' he said slowly.

'Anaemia,' echoed Dan. 'What's that?'

'He said . . . something lacking in her blood.'

'But that's all right, surely,' answered the boy desperately, 'they can . . . can replace what is lacking?'

'Not with this kind, son' Johnny replied.

Startled by being called 'son' - it had been a long time since his father had used the affectionate word - Dan looked at his face; what he saw was naked pain and despair. Not knowing what to say, he muttered that he would get some kindlings, and rushed outside. Passing the window he glimpsed Johnny; he was slumped at the table with his head in his hands.

'He does care,' he thought in wonder. 'He is terrified to lose her, just as terrified as I am! Then why, why doesn't he show it? Why does he not tell her he loves her? Why does he have to hide away from us both?'

He sat in the barn until his thoughts had grown calmer. Finally he said to himself, 'Why don't *I* tell her either? I'm just as bad as he is!' In some strange way, though, he felt comforted. When he returned to the house there was no sign of his father, but his mother was moving about slowly, making the supper as usual. She said nothing about the doctor.

It was from that day that he found himself beginning to think seriously about old Murray's words. What he loved most in the world he could not have. He now faced the fact that he was likely to lose his mother; the thought of staying here with his father alone was unthinkable. The farm was not big enough for both of them. Perhaps after all he should prepare himself for the thought of leaving; perhaps one day he should try to find freedom to be himself, to live his life as he wanted it. And one day he would come back, back to the glen and to Achnagreine; and the land would be his, truly his own as his brother had wished it to be all those years ago.

All the same, he did not reach a decision for some time. There were days when he accepted that he would go; and he would almost pluck up courage to seek out Mr Murray and tell him he would sit for the bursary after all. Equally, on other days the very idea of going to the city, enduring the long years there, seemed like utter madness. How could he bear to be away from everything that he cared about? Often he was simply in doubt, trapped as it were in the deep pool of his own confusion. Perhaps it would be better to find work somewhere else in the glen - that way he would not lose everything. Underneath all the uncertainty was one clear thought; he had to escape, even for a time, from the domination of his father. He had to be himself.

Then came a day when Rena, his mother, was finally beaten. Dead tired, weary of the unending struggle, she took to her bed, and slept for several days. Coming home from school, everything seemed altogether empty and cheerless to Dan; the very air seemed strange. In the deserted kitchen there was no welcoming smell of baking. He now had to cook for his father; their meals were eaten in almost complete silence, and Dan dreaded them. His mother ate little, mainly tea and fruit; sometimes, though, she would ask him to cook fish for her.

She did not remain in bed after the first few days; revived to some extent, she got up and, still a prisoner in her room, began to paint again. It had been a long time since she had last touched her brushes; it was as though she poured into the new canvases all of the mingled love and longing and sadness that were bound within her. Rich as the paintings were with detail and colour, there was yet a kind of jaggedness, seen especially in the trees and the skies, that seemed to reflect something of her own inner pain. She moved into Dan's room to paint the view up to Beinn Dobhran, her favourite of all as it was Dan's too. He was not allowed to see it until it was finished; when he did, he could not help throwing his arms around her in sheer joy, laughing with delight, proud of her, amazed that despite her weakness her gift was still so great. As she hugged him, a golden light caught her thin face from the evening sun. He knelt by her side, as if begging a favour:

'Mother, I want you to know something . . . I'm working for the bursary, to go to university.'

Her face lit up and her tired eyes shone as she held him close and said: 'That's wonderful, Danny. And I know you will do well!' Then, after a moment, she gently teased him, ruffling his hair, 'but you'll have to work hard - not so many hours up in the woods any more. It'll be the midnight oil from now on!' She laughed and hugged him again.

What meant more to him than anything else was that they had become close again. Somehow the spontaneous delight which the painting had released in him had also broken down his stiffness; he realised it was he who had made the gulf which had in recent months grown up between them, his growing up which had shut her out.

All those years his mother had been there, ready to welcome him when he came home, but he had not properly seen her; he had taken her for granted. Now he determined it would be different. And he found himself doing the things he had almost forgotten - on his way home from school, he would pick a bag of hazelnuts to lay on her table as she lay sleeping. Or he would make her an especially tempting supper, and sit by her, telling her all the day's happenings, while she ate it. He spent as much time with her as his homework would permit.

For a time, during a spell of perfect autumn weather, she seemed to rally, to regain a little of her former vitality. Dan was ready to make the most of it. On a golden day of early October sunshine, he persuaded her to come up with him to Donnie's Pool. It was a Saturday, and he had worked hard at his homework all morning; then he had made a picnic for the two of them, with all the things she liked best. It was as though she had become the child, he thought; all she had once given him he now delighted in finding for her.

As they sat there together in the late afternoon light, he had taken her hand and said gently 'You're a lot better, mother. By the time spring comes you'll be well.'

He saw her lips trembling. For a few moments she did not reply; then, in a small voice she had said 'Don't, Danny; don't break my heart by saying such things. I only wish with all my heart you were right. And I had . . . I had longed to see you through university. It was Andrew's dream too, you know.'

She was silent then, and sat holding his hand, while a pain that was almost physical passed through his whole body. He could not answer.

She continued, 'But we'll be good to each other.'

At that moment he thought of his father. He and his mother were now so close; sometimes it seemed as if Johnny had ceased to exist.

There were times when he could feel sorry for him. He and his mother would spend an hour or more in her room, talking of many things, looking at her paintings perhaps, sharing deeply now that all was well between them once again; then his father would come in, expecting his supper; as always he would seem withdrawn, in a sense threatening; Dan knew that he could never overcome the edge of fear he felt whenever Johnny was there. He was shut out, a stranger; and while Dan blamed him for it, he still at times could feel pity for his loneliness. After all these years, he still recalled that time, after his grandmother's death, when his father had for once opened up his inner self to him; he could still see him kneeling by his bedside and hear him say: 'Here I am at last, talking to you'.

'Why, why, why,' he cried to himself, 'can he not do it again? What is wrong with him; how did he come to be like this? Is my mother dying of a blood disease or of a broken heart? But then, is his heart not broken too? And whose fault is it but his own?' It was all beyond Dan. He felt trapped, baffled; he would never be able to understand.

Then there was the question of the land. Dan felt that there was another world which was his father's, a world he was not allowed to enter. Although he helped around the farm, and indeed there was often far too much for him to do, he was very aware that in a sense he was shut out; this land, to him more precious than gold, was possessed by Johnny. He longed for the day when it would be his own.

His father did not once mention the exam; Dan did not tell him about it, but he knew that Johnny would have heard. The thought came to him that his father would think that Dan had given up and was leaving, as it were beaten, driven away; that he, Johnny, had won. Then he dismissed the thought as unfair. He did not really believe it was like this.

So the winter went past; Dan had never known one so dreary. His mother never left her room now; the short-lived improvement was over. As spring came, what hurt Dan most was the awareness that the house was not clean any more. In the old days, he knew, he would

69

never have noticed; now he began to see cobwebs in the rooms, and was aware of a general air of untidiness and neglect. As he came up the glen from school, he could see the housewives busily engaged in the annual ritual of spring-cleaning, and he would recall the joy his mother had taken in her freshly-washed blankets and curtains, the spotless floors and polished brasses. His heart felt like lead.

But one day a girl started up the track to Achnagreine. She had two big cases in her hands and she walked slowly, her gaze fixed on the ground. Dan went down nervously to help her, whistling because he was shy and had no idea what to say. He took the cases and then walked a little ahead of her. She was Catriona Morrison, and she had come because Johnny had suddenly announced that the house was going to wreck and ruin. Her parents were from the Isle of Lewis, but after a short time in Glasgow they had settled in Abercree. Dan scrutinised her discreetly while they were having a cup of tea in his mother's room. She was pale, and had thin white hands rather like his mother's. Her long brown hair flowed down her back, thick and glossy. They stood together at the window; Johnny, digging in the garden, looked up and saw them; he raised a hand in greeting.

'Your father?' she asked. In her voice was a kind of music that he did not miss, the lilt of Gaelic.

'Aye,' he answered sharply, not looking at her, annoyed with himself that he had somehow allowed anger into his reply. 'You're not seeing the place at its best yet,' he went on quickly, 'the green's not back yet. The hills are a bit colourless at this time.'

She laughed lightly. 'I know,' she said, 'we have a few round Abercree, you know.'

She wasn't really laughing at him, he decided; there was a friendly glint in her eyes. All the same he felt himself beginning to redden. He was glad to go over and open the door for Corrie; the collie growled ominously on seeing a stranger. But she spoke gently in Gaelic, and the dog relaxed, even let her stroke his head. Maybe a token,

70

he thought, of her acceptance at Achnagreine? Rena, his mother, managed later to come downstairs in her dressing-gown, to show Catriona the cupboards and drawers where things were kept; after Dan left them, he heard them talking and laughing together as if they had known each other for ages; he felt his spirits rise as they had not done for a very long time. He knew things were going to be better, especially perhaps for his mother. Catriona seemed a quietly confident person; although she must only be a couple of years older than himself, she seemed many years older in maturity.

She was to have the little spare room across the landing from his own. It smelled a little of damp, he noticed, as he set her cases down; but she laughed and said it would be fine for her. Even Johnny came in from his work earlier than usual, put his head round the door and said to Catriona with a shy smile:

'Och, well, you seem to be settling in grand.'

At dinner, she chattered to Dan and his father about Lewis, about Glasgow, as well as about her family and - as she put it - the hundred and forty-three cousins she still had on the islands; she told them how she missed the ceilidhs, how she loved and hated the life all at the same time and never knew whether she wanted to go back or not.

But it was the farming Johnny wanted to know about - how many sheep they had had on the croft, how hard was it to make a living there? Catriona ended by laughing at the seriousness of the questions; Johnny looked at her a little startled, but she told him she had been too young when they left the island to know much of croft life; what she remembered best were the winter gales and the slates rattling, and in the summer going for water with buckets - and finding wild orchids on the moors.

'Do you like orchids?' Dan said quickly.

'There's nothing more beautiful,' she answered simply.

'They were my granny's favourite flower' - he felt himself begin to redden as he spoke, and bent quickly to eat again; there was still a burning at the back of his eyes when he thought of her. He could not say any more.

'Catriona is good for us all' he told himself as he went to bed that night. First, she would be company for his mother, and would be able to cook dainty meals which he himself could not do properly. It would make his own life much easier too; sometimes he had difficulty getting his homework done with all the extra work; his father, for all his faults never a mean man, insisted that Rena had a fire in her room all the time; that was only one of the jobs which fell to his lot. But the really important thing, he felt, was that she did not seem the least bit in awe of his father - maybe the silent meals would even be a thing of the past.

And so it proved. He no longer dreaded coming home to find the empty silence of the kitchen, his mother lonely and depressed upstairs, his father withdrawn and tense. Catriona wasted no time in tackling the work - Dan noticed the well-scrubbed doorstep, the spotless curtains, the smell of polish on the furniture - and it did his heart good. Before going off to begin his homework he would sit talking to her as she went briskly here and there, preparing things for the meal. She was full of fun, and was forever pulling his leg about housework, telling him with a sarcastic grin how impressed she was at the tidiness of his room. But she wanted to know a host of things about the glen - where his favourite places were; whether there were eagles (she recalled seeing them as a child in Lewis); how much Gaelic he knew; whether he had heard this story or that, or knew certain Gaelic songs. She told him also of her life in Glasgow, of the ceilidhs they used to go to, where most of the people you met were themselves Lewis exiles and knew all the same people. He told her of the bursary he was working for, and she was full of enthusiasm.

'You must go to Glasgow!' she said excitedly. 'It's the best city for Highlanders - and after all you can easily come home for the holidays; it's not as though you'll be away for ever!'

The months went on and New Year came again. A New Year when it seemed to him they were all so happy together that he began to have serious doubts about going away at all. Looking back to the previous year, Dan could now scarcely believe they were the same family. All the old friends came for the celebration - old Calum from up at Camus Lurgan, Alasdair the roadman bearing his beloved fiddle, Jessie and Kirsty Maclean, two sisters who sang Gaelic duets, Iain with his melodeon, Peter the post with his mouth organ. They even cleared the floor and had an eightsome reel. And his mother was downstairs, looking so much better and happier that when he caught sight of her face he wanted to cry for sheer joy. Best of all was that Johnny was sitting beside her, holding her hand. When the glasses were passed round, he did not even object when Dan calmly helped himself to one. He had not felt so happy, he thought, since he was a small child. This was New Year as it should be.

He could not get to sleep that night for thinking of his father. What an enigma the man was! When would he ever understand him? This silent war that went on between the two of them - how much he longed for it to be over. Sometimes he would have an urge to go to him and simply tell him he loved him. But what would come of it? He felt that the answer lay with Johnny himself. It was surely *he* who had built up this strong dyke around himself, not to mention the precious land which he so jealously guarded, and so only *he* could break it down. There were times when Dan would pluck up courage to go to him with an idea, perhaps of something they could do together, or someone they might visit; always, though, he seemed to be left feeling that his timing had been wrong; he would vow never to be so stupid again. He would swing this way and that, between hatred and love. At times he doubted whether his father's friendly overture on the night of his grandmother's death had ever happened at all.

'Dan, you need to get away,' Catriona suddenly said to him one day when he was staring out of the window, his thoughts far away. The snow was beginning to melt; soon it would be lambing time again, and he could expect to hear his father's voice in the early dark, calling for him to help. The girl sat down beside him and he noticed the red-gold sheen that lit her hair as she looked at him, her head to one side, her expression half comical, half gentle.

'I worry about you, Dan, you know. Half the time you're away in your own world and you shut folk out. You're a bit like your father, if you ask me.'

He turned round with an expression of horror so that she laughed out loud. 'Och, I said it to annoy you . . . but there's truth in it! You're a right pair, the two of you. It's not easy, believe me, living under the same roof with you both. You're like two strange collies, circling each other the whole time, waiting for the chance to have a nip at each other. No wonder your poor mother's tired out!'

Dan looked round at Catriona sharply, shaken by what she had said.

'D'you blame me too then?'

'Yes, I do!' she retorted with feeling. 'You certainly don't make things any easier. You take your mother's side in every single thing, just because of your war with your father.'

'That's not fair, Catriona. I do it to protect her . . . she's had to put up with him for so long. He acted as if he was God Almighty when I was younger; he thought he could rule us all. I won't let him any more, and he knows it.'

She nodded, her eyes searching his face. He felt a sudden heat in himself, that burned and passed. He must not! But she was beautiful; he had been aware of it from the first day, and told himself sternly that he must suppress the flame in his being. Deep down he knew that he had fallen in love; he was determined all the same not to acknowledge the fact. She was more than two years older than himself; he was still only a schoolboy. How could she possibly take him seriously? Thus he crushed his feelings, not daring to allow them to develop further. One moment he would attempt to deny their very existence, the next he would be desolate to think she had come just as he was about to leave. He had never felt more con-fused.

He sat the bursary exam. He had worked feverishly, sometimes through the entire night, in the lamplight of his room, until his eyes were badly strained and he was near exhaustion. When he came home that day, Catriona, full of questions, was eager to know how it had gone. He simply could not say; he told her quietly that they would have to wait and see, and he went to lie on his bed so that he might attempt to gather his muddled thoughts. His mother and Catriona. What exactly did he want? Was it worth the price - escaping from his father, to lose them both? Had Catriona been right in what she said, that he was to blame as well as his father? But the thought of leaving here! He would come back, though . . . just three or four years in the city. But would it be too late? He didn't know, he didn't know! If only someone could advise him! If only he could see into the future! Perhaps the best thing would be to put it out of his mind until he knew the results of the bursary.

At last the papers came. It was a Saturday; and for that whole day he kept them unopened in his room, saying nothing to anybody. He had put them into a drawer and in the afternoon had gone away by himself, right up into the corrie below Beinn Dobhran. It was a still day; not a breath of wind, no movement except that of the sheep as they passed below him among the pas-ture, mainly the grass that grew among the heather. And a single buzzard high above him, come down from the sharp-cut edges of the Beinn, mewing with a cry which surprisingly seemed no stronger than that of a mouse. A long glide as it circled, two wing beats to keep height, then the long glide again. He sat for a time beside one of the dark lochans, trying to find stones that could skip over the water, but all he found was shingle and rough edges of quartz and granite.

'What on earth am I doing up here,' he asked himself, 'running away from the answer?' The question came into his mind before he seemed to have given it conscious thought. What was the point of torturing himself? He had to know! Yet there was a part of him that was scared - for so long he had been at a kind of cross-roads, waiting and wondering; now it was out of his hands, the decision made. True, but did he really know what he wanted? It was as though the child inside himself was frightened, not knowing. He got up and started back the way he had come. And as he crossed one of the deep channels that linked the lochs, flowing black and clear as liquid smoky quartz, he caught sight of a young fish darting under the bank. Only a second and it was gone, yet somehow it set him thinking. The fish would go down to the sea, leave the glen river until the water had turned bitter with salt; but it would come back! It would find a way past the nets on the estuary, back to this place, the beginning. He knew before he opened the envelope what his answer would be.

Chapter 9

Dan shivered. It was cold here in the trees' shadow, as the wind gusted over the barrow and hissed into the wood behind. He would have to start walking again. There seemed to be so little time; he had taken perhaps an hour to reach this far from the farm. To think how fast he once had run here! But he did not want to leave this special place - not yet, at least; there was too much to remember. And having come so far in his journey of remembering, he was determined to go on.

That day when the bursary results came was still as clear in his memory as if it had been last week. Catriona had danced with him round the kitchen. He had had a great urge to kiss her, but he had refrained. His father had shaken his hand; even he, that day, had been unable to keep from smiling.

'Well, you're the cleverest of the Drummonds,' he had said, 'but don't let it go to your head!'

His mother, who should have been the first to know, was the last. That would need time. He went in to her room, the paper half-crumpled in his hand; he saw her turned away on one side as she slept, heard her soft breathing. Her little paraffin lamp still burned by the bedside; the book she had been reading had slid down to the floor. He looked out of the window in the growing dusk at the field that ran down to the Lodge; the ruins, he thought, were as dead and silent as his grandmother. He knelt softly by the bed and reached for the hand that was curled around the covers. She wakened up slowly, saw him at once and smiled sleepily.

'I won the bursary, mother,' he whispered.

'Of course you did, Danny,' she said, and opened her arms to hold him.

'I want you to know something, though.' It was not easy for him to speak; he had to fight to get the words out. 'I'll come back, the minute you need me . . . if you . . . if you're not better.' He did not dare say it any other way, but she understood; she held his head between her hands, and made him look at her.

'Listen, Danny,' she said urgently. 'You've been here when I needed you most. All of these years. But when I'm . . . when I'm really ill, I won't be myself any more and I don't want you to see it. It would break you. Please . . . I'd rather you remembered.' Her voice failed and she hugged him tightly to her.

Never had he loved her so much. And in his heart he cried out again and again: 'God, if you're there, if you're hearing me now, listen - don't take her away!'

But the summer came and went and she was worse. The weather was sultry; her room was too hot, and she could get no rest. Dan could see that his father was frightened; he was short with Dan and even irritable with Catriona. He sat far longer than usual at the kitchen table, looking away from them into the yard, his face grey and drawn. Dan suddenly saw him looking much older, his hair almost all white now, the furrows across his brow deep-ploughed. The walls he had built around himself now seemed higher than ever; in his grief he had retreated even further into himself. In near desperation, Dan would think back to that one night when the iron gates had been opened, when he had allowed the light as it were to fall on his inmost soul, allowing his son to glimpse the guilt he felt over over his dead mother and Andrew. Yet he had not learned; he was still doing the same things, was still closing himself so that none could reach him. And soon it would again be too late - Rena would be gone.

Dan was at times half crazed with a mixture of pity and frustration. Before he left Achnagreine, he determined to find a way of breaking that wall, for his mother's sake if not for his own. Again and again he had sought the answer and had come no closer. On those hot, airless nights he had lain awake and heard his mother coughing; his thoughts gave him no rest either, and he fell into an uneasy sleep just before it was time to get up. His mother began another canvas but again would not let him see it until it was finished. He had to help her over to the other side of the room and he dreaded this; each time it seemed to take an eternity. As he supported her he would lay his head gently against her shoulder, feeling her ribs, her frail body that was turning thin as a bird's. Once she had run with him into the fields above Balree to pick mushrooms, played hide-and-seek in the woods around the farm and he had believed she would never grow old; she was eternal, strong and full of laughter. Now, sometimes, she could not even summon up the strength to talk to him; she just smiled with a kind of twisting of the mouth, and pain would surge through him as he looked away.

Catriona asked him suddenly one day whether he had found lodgings in Glasgow; his mind was far away and he had trouble in focusing his thoughts. He did not reply. He went out quickly and ran up to his refuge, the barrow at the edge of the wood; in the dark shade of the pines he lay down, smelling the moss, watching the birds moving restlessly among the trees, listening to the running of the stream that had shrunk to almost nothing. And he cried.

At home he began to make preparations for leaving, far earlier than he needed to. Not because he wanted to go, but because he was frightened. He did not know what would happen next; it seemed to give him the chance to have things ordered, to feel himself at least master of the small world of what he had, when all that was inside him had been ransacked and burnt, left in ruins. His mother was clearly getting worse. One day the doctor came and Dan waited down in the kitchen for a long time, cutting aimlessly at a piece of wood with his penknife. When the man came down heavily from her room at last, he touched Dan's shoulder gently; he had known them for a long time.

'Is she any better?' A plea, not a question.

'I'm afraid not, Dan,' the answer came in a quiet voice; the boy turned to look into the fire. There was no more to be said.

But his goodbye had been said already. She had finished her last canvas two days ago, and was happy about it. It was the view down to the Lodge and the hills beyond, with the light as it came in the early morning. He had held her hand and simply sat there, nodding and smiling in appreciation, filled with gladness for her that she had managed to complete her task, filled too with love and grief that broke him in pieces like a leaf in a river's flood. She had tried to raise herself in the bed, but could not; she attempted to laugh but started to cough instead. Then, brokenly:

'This one is for you, Danny. You are to keep it. Always.'

He could not speak. He would never forget her. As she now smiled, she was suddenly as she once had been - the thinness that had changed her beauty was gone, and she was mother, the mother he had known from the beginning.

Now he was ready; it was done. His room was almost bare, a dark shell that possessed him no longer. The two big cases stood there, waiting for him, on the day the thunderstorm came. The fields had turned ill and red-brown, sick with the drought. Between the pools of the burn there ran thin serpents of water, a mere trickle. Dan watched the yard, the rough pasture that ran as far up as the first screes, the grey dome of Beinn Dobhran, as suddenly the darkness seemed to rear like wild horses over the glen, orange and purple masses of cloud as the lightning flickered down and a great roll of thunder went on and on. He opened the window and put his head out; drops of rain as big as grapes soaked it in a moment; he closed his eyes and let the water run down his face.

'Dan!' It was his father, down below. 'Help me cover the bales!'

It did not register with him for a moment; it was as if he did not understand the question. He kept looking

80

down dumbly at the white, upturned face; then his father turned and ran to the back of the yard where the dry bales were stacked. Dan ran downstairs; he opened the back door and stood there for a moment as the huge drops splashed across his hands and shoulders. Then he was running over the ground that was dancing with silver, until he was standing above his father's bent back.

'Father!'

He had not heard; he was still struggling to move the bales.

'Father!' he tried again. He must have heard; he was just not listening to him. Dan could not bear it. Blindly, in sheer desperation, he pulled his father up with all his might, to face him. The face seemed empty; the expression changed to one of utter shock as Dan struck the pale cheek. A red weal spread as he looked with horror at what he had done. But he was past caring now.

'Father!' he shouted again, half sobbing. 'Go, go now - let me do this. Go to mother, for God's sake! Don't waste another minute; tell her, tell her you love her! Don't leave her as you left granny! Can't you see? There's so little time left!'

He was really sobbing now, broken, the dam burst. Nothing mattered any more except that Johnny should go to her. And when he looked up, he had indeed gone. The drought, the thirst, finished. He heard their voices in her room as he came downstairs with his cases, quiet and close. That was all that mattered.

Catriona was standing by the fire when he went in; she looked startled as she saw the cases and realised he was leaving. He smiled gently at her; then he went over to her, kissed her softly and touched her hair, as he so often yearned to do.

'I'm going, Catriona. Now, tonight, I've finished everything I needed to do. But I'll be back; I promise you I'll be back.'

Chapter 10

The old man smiled to himself as his thoughts went back to that day, more than sixty years ago. In the end, he reflected, the circle had been complete; he had gone in peace.

He got up from his seat on the ancient mound, and moved into the shelter of the wood. The streams were choked; it seemed that they gossiped to each other as they flowed down to join the burn that passed the farm and Shian, sounding for all the world like the voices of the old women as they came out of church and stood talking together in their tight black circles.

He had lost the glen of his childhood, he mused as he walked, lost it and then found it again. He had discovered what lay beyond the ring of hills which had enclosed his early world, had as it were reached up to pick his own Eden fruit, and found that it was the trees of home which bore the apple, however bitter, that alone could assuage his thirst and give peace to his heart.

He left Achnagreine knowing full well that his mother had precious few days left. But his farewells had been said; he knew that and so did she. He remembered her as she had been, all that had nourished his childhood. Now there was no choice but to turn away, all the rich memories stored in his heart. He told himself that he must grieve no more; rivers of mourning had flowed out of him already; now he must look to the future. And one day he would return.

Glasgow. As he turned his thoughts to that period of his life, he found a strange thing - his mind would not function in its normal way. Whereas the memories of the glen in his early years were as clear as if the events had happened yesterday, the sequence absolutely fixed in his mind, of Glasgow he could recapture only a kind of kaleidoscope of impressions, with a few outstanding happenings etched clearly in his memory. For example, he could recall little of the journey south - only that the hills became noticeably lower as the train snaked its way southwards. At one point a little boy in the compartment had suddenly noticed Dan opposite him and had shrieked:

'Look at his funny hair!'

The child had been duly reprimanded and smacked; but Dan had all at once become aware of his shabby clothes and luggage, and had shrunk back into his corner, overcome with embarrassment. He remembered too that, as they neared the city, the miles and miles of drab tenements - grey-black buildings where surely the sun's rays never penetrated - seemed to go on for ever. There was so little green left; the few trees looked almost black, and he fancied they fought for breath among all the grime-laden stones. As the train passed slowly by, he remembered catching sight of groups of ragged children watching it, young girls carrying younger children in their arms - the face of poverty as he had never seen it until then.

Of his arrival he remembered little except that all seemed to be bustle and activity - and noise; he never became used to the city's noise, of shouting, trams and motors. A flurry of grey doves, he recalled, had risen up around him as he heaved his heavy cases out of the train. What struck him was that everyone but himself seemed to know where they were going.

More impressions surged back as Dan began to concentrate his mind on that far-away time. He remembered his room. He had asked for one where he could cook his own food; it was cheaper than the more usual 'lodgings with full board'. In a dingy tenement, considered superior because the walls of the 'close' were tiled, it was up four flights, at the very top of the building, and contained a small iron bed, a table and chair, a large cupboard and a single gas ring. The high ceiling made it seem cold and unfriendly; the only consolation he found on that first night was a tiny skylight on the landing, through which he could just make out the stars.

He remembered his landlady. Even now, after much experience of life, he marvelled that anyone could have shown so little interest in another human being, especially in one so obviously at sea as he had been. She had her own family and was totally immersed in her own affairs and theirs; she found out nothing about him, and came to see him each week only to collect the rent. If I died tonight, Dan would sometimes think, she would never know until rent day; even then she would care only about the nuisance it would cause. He knew that he had been singularly unlucky; other students seemed to have landladies who cared about them. From time to time in chance encounters, usually in the small shops, he would meet people who exhibited some of the warmth for which this city was generally known.

The loneliness, especially in the first week or two before classes began, almost crushed him at times. He wondered how he could possibly survive it until term ended; then he remembered that he would not be going home for the holidays - how could he bear even to think of New Year in the glen now? That was what he most remembered - the loneliness. And the dirt and deprivation. It was the beginning of the Depression, and groups of thin, hopeless-looking men could be seen standing at every street corner. Pale women carried their babies tightly wrapped in shawls tied around them. Ragged children, many with the leg deformities he had been told denoted rickets, were everywhere.

He remembered the struggle to survive on his bursary. He had in fact been awarded two, the extra one being given to certain students from the Highlands and Islands. In addition, he had a few pounds which a cousin in Australia had left to him a couple of years before. He had been determined to manage without asking his father for a penny; but Johnny had insisted on giving him ten pounds - a princely sum for those days - on the day the news of the bursary came. He realised he was going to need every single penny. All the same, it had not been so very many years since students from the glens used to go to university with a sack of oatmeal to last them the whole term; he was infinitely better off. He determined to live largely on porridge and potatoes; what else after all could he hope to cook on one gas ring? And he must forego the luxury of taking a tram. Yet one of his few happy memories was of a day when he had, in the teeming rain, got on to a tram. It was absolutely empty, and the conductor was standing by the door lustily singing a Gaelic song. Dan, his heart leaping with delight, could not resist joining in, and they finished the verse in duet. The conductor, equally delighted, greeted him in fluent Gaelic. Dan went past his stop in the excitement of finding that Duncan came from Skye, from the next township to that in which his grandmother Eliza had grown up.

After perhaps a week, on a day when he had spoken to no-one and felt he could not bear the loneliness another moment, he decided he would go into a pub. The very idea made him nervous; he knew too that he could not hope to eat if he spent money on whisky, but in desperation he shrugged the knowledge off. It was a Saturday night and he sat on his own, drinking his whisky faster because he had nobody to talk to. All around him were voices, ugly voices of working men, arguing, sometimes shouting, looking angrily at him - or so he imagined - if they caught him looking at them too intently. The whisky burned his throat; he did not like it, simply hoped it would dull his pain for even a little. Nobody spoke to him. Suddenly he noticed a man who looked like his father; guilt washed over him at the thought of what his parents would think if they were to see him in a place like this; not only that, but he reckoned the whisky was costing him as much as a week's ration of oatmeal and potatoes. A fight broke out noisily at the other end of the bar; he finished his drink hastily and began to edge out. The bar was closing, and in a tight scrum of feet and sour voices and smoke they were all pushed out on to the street. But he felt warmed and relaxed now; then suddenly, as in a dream, he seemed to see his own feet walking down in twilight from Beinn Dobhran to the yard at Achnagreine. It was a long way home. A hard key in his pocket, to admit him to his cold empty room; girls going home with laughing faces, protecting their hair with shawls as they half-ran in the rain along the glistening pavements. He did not go in a straight line; his hands were stuck into his pockets; his head hung so that the horizontal rain did not touch his face. Nobody could see that he was crying.

He decided after that that he would not go into a pub again; instead, he would buy a small bottle of whisky - the gill size - and drink it only when things got too bad. He bought the bottle. Then came the day he would never forget. Dan could not remember now how long it was after he had left the glen, only that it was the day before classes were to begin. As usual he had spoken to nobody all day. A deep depression had hung over him from the moment he had wakened up; he had been unable to banish thoughts of his mother for even a moment. Reaching near-desperation, he had gone for the bottle of whisky and drunk the entire gill. Soon after he had finished it, his landlady shouted that he had a visitor. It was Davie Shaw, a boy who had been a year ahead of him at school and was starting his second year at university. He was shy, turning his cap round and round in his hands.

'I . . . I came back from the glen today, Dan,' he said quietly. 'Your father asked me to tell you . . . to say that your mother died this morning.'

How cold and final it sounded! Not that he blamed Davie; he felt sorry for him, having to bear such a message. There was silence as Dan struggled to remain calm. But had he not known all day? Not once had she left his thoughts. So she was gone! All he wanted was for Davie to go and leave him to his grief, but he did not know how to send him away. He felt awkward too because he knew his breath must smell of whisky; not only that, but when the boys at school had laughed at Davie because he was old-fashioned, religious, he had often joined in. Oh, he had been nice enough when they were alone together, but not in the pack. All these thoughts surged through his head as they stood there in what must have been a long silence. Then, keeping his voice as steady as he could, he said:

'Sit down, Davie. And thank you for coming to tell me.'

The boy sat down uncertainly on the only chair. Then, looking out of the window, Dan went on:

'I came away early, you know. It was the right time and I don't regret it. You won't understand, but in the end I was glad. There was nothing more I could have done.'

He knew his voice was slurred; he knew he was concentrating too hard on his words and he knew that Davie knew this. But what did anything matter now? If only he would go! But he sat there looking dumbly up at him, so Dan continued:

'You probably think I'm callous . . . but she began . . . began dying a long time ago - and she was tired.'

For a moment he saw her there, pale and drawn, at the kitchen table; his voice caught on a nail-sharp edge, but he did not break.

'Only at the end I saw it and . . . and I gave everything I had. That was why I went away, Davie; there was nothing left to give.'

He looked intently at Davie and the boy's glance shifted.

'What about . . . the funeral, then?'

Dan turned away and leant his elbows on the window sill.

'You won't understand.' He almost groaned. 'Nobody will understand.'

He was not simply speaking to Davie, but to himself and to all the ghosts who asked him the same question. Perhaps one day he would not understand himself; but for now, at this moment he knew exactly what he was doing, and he knew what the answer must be.

'I'm not going to the funeral. There's no need.'

'But Dan, think of your father!' the boy burst out.

That made him angry. 'For once I'm thinking of myself and not my father,' he said. 'After all the years he hasn't thought of me - no, nor of my mother. He's the one who needs to make his peace with her, not me. I said goodbye all right, not at some empty hole, like on the day my granny was buried, but at her bedside, when she was still alive. Then it meant something. It was telling her I loved her, knowing she heard me.'

He was almost breathless by now and he lowered his hands, and then put his head down on the sill as if in prayer.

'Something of the glen is dead now, Davie. I said good-bye to them both and....I'm here. One day I will go back, but the wounds have to heal. I have a lot to learn before then.'

'Don't fail her then, Dan,' he heard Davie say softly, but he did not raise his head. 'Don't lose yourself here, in this dead place. Too many have done that - got lost and never gone back. And Dan - don't lose your faith, for her sake.'

When Dan at last looked up, he had gone. Then he could let the tears come.

He forced himself the next day to go and find his way around the university. Fighting to keep afloat in the sea of misery which threatened at times to overwhelm him, he went up to the quadrangles and the high towers of dark stone; he gazed at the ornate windows, the tall pillars, and felt guilty as he recognised in himself a flash of pride that he was here, in this place of ancient learning. There was even a kind of beauty in the sunlight shining on the pearl drops of rain on the iron railings; he had never thought to see beauty in any city. Later, in the huge English class, he felt poor and shabby again; everyone else seemed so poised, so well dressed. But as time went on he was to meet many others from the glens and the islands, to feel at home in the endless discussions and arguments, to form his own opinions with confidence. But it took a long time.

All these years later Dan remembered little of it, certainly no kind of sequence; the days of his first term were a blur, made up of classes in which he struggled to understand, failed to write fast enough, struggled again at home to make some sense of his notes, tried to feed himself adequately, and had endless cups of tea with a handful of new friends who were as much at sea as himself. He told no-one at all about his mother. When the misery became too bad, he drank whisky. It helped at night but made the mornings much worse. And then he was hungry because he dared not spend too much on food.

Once, desperate to see some green, he went to the park. Down from the dark castle of the university and into this strange world with a dirty black river flowing through; he leaned over the bridge, trying not think of another river. Old men looked curiously at him as he passed, he fancied with a touch of fear. He had seen the same look as girls turned away their eyes from him or crossed the street as he came near. He wanted to shout aloud that he would do them no harm, there was no need to be afraid of him. This park seemed to him an unreal place, a world that did not belong to the world of reality. Someone had told him he ought to go there because it was 'like the country'. But not to him. It only made him all the more restless and frustrated; to compare it to the real countryside he had known all his life was unthinkable. It might be fine for them - he thought of the lovers he saw on many of the benches around him. *I know what it's like for me - I am like a foal that is given an edge of grass to run in when it has remembered fields without end.*

The days went on into autumn. Dan recalled a day when he saw a chestnut tree at the edge of the park. The sight of the shiny mahogany chestnuts was almost like a physical pain. There were times when the struggle not to think, not to remember, seemed almost to drain away all the strength he had. And while he could manage to blot out the memories - of his mother, Catriona, Achnagreine and the glen - during waking times, in sleep he was defeated. Dan now realised that he still remembered some of his dreams more vividly than he remembered his life in the city.

In one of these, his father came and wakened him up, smiled, and told him they were going home. They went by train, but the houses went on for mile after mile, so that he began to be afraid that they would never escape. Then Johnny told him to go to sleep; and in the dream he put his arm around Dan, so that he felt secure and happy. When he opened his eyes they had arrived, but strangely they were coming running down to Achnagreine from the hill above, and his mother was waiting for them, waving from the back door.

Another dream had recurred and recurred. Again he sat in the train, a ticket held tightly in his hand on which was written 'Achnagreine'. Suddenly from the window he would see the farm, set in its own place beneath Beinn Dobhran; but all around were roads and tenements and factories. He would beat against the glass to get free, until the picture misted and he awoke. But the horror of it would hang like a dark cloud over him all day.

Although lostness and loneliness were the predominant memories of that part of his life, Dan found that individual acts of kindness still remained. Like the time he had met old Mrs Dean. Of all the people he had rubbed shoulders with as they came and went in his landlady's house, only she had taken any interest in him; the others, like his landlady, had smiled at him and asked him how he liked Glasgow and then listened to nothing of his reply. They talked without listening, looked without seeing. Mrs Dean was different. She asked him about his home, his studies; seeing perhaps something of the isolation he was feeling, she invited him to come for supper the next night. He went shyly; but in the warmth and kindness of the welcome she and her husband gave him, he relaxed. Apart from his cousin Alec, they were the only city people he had ever known.

A letter came from Catriona. He recognised her writing from the shopping lists he had seen her write. He could not bring himself to open it at once; it appeared to him more significant and in a way more dangerous than any he had received before, and he wanted to think. He had heard nothing from his father since he left; he had met nobody from the glen apart from Davie. Since then his world had changed; it seemed that the light had gone. What had his father thought of his failure to come home? What had Catriona thought? Was she perhaps writing to tell him she was leaving Achnagreine? Or had something else happened - his father? He took the letter with him to university and felt it in his breast pocket; he held it in his hands at the lecture hall as he sat alone; he looked at it, as if somehow he could divine its contents. In the evening, on impulse he went again to a pub, taking it with him. He sat at a table by himself, looking at no-one, drinking quickly. When after a time he felt as if cocooned in his own world, warmed inside and fortified against possible shock, he at last opened the letter, tearing at it with clumsy fingers. His hands were trembling, his heart beating fast. But there was after all no condemnation; just the prayer of them all that he was well and that he would be looked after and upheld. No empty words to say that his mother had died peacefully, that the funeral had been good, that people had been kind . . . just suddenly...

'When the spring comes I'll go up to the wood above Balree and pick some primroses. I know they were your mother's favourite flower; and it's one of the places I could imagine her best, Dan, among the trees in their fresh green and the spring all around. I'll have them on the table in the kitchen, with fresh water each day to keep them as long as possible'.

He folded the letter and held it in his hands and breathed deeply in relief. It was all right! She did not think him callous, did not blame him for his failure to come home. She understood.

He recalled another dream. His mother came to his bedside and spoke to him gently, telling him they would go home. It seemed everything was ready in his room; all his belongings packed and standing in the middle of the floor. Then, as if for an eternity, they were walking through the streets, in all the traffic, the smoke and the noise; his feet were bare. All at once his mother was not with him any more, and he was calling, calling for her above the noise of the trams and the newspaper sellers and the men with their barrows of fruit. But they did not listen and it was no good - she was gone. As he continued to call her name, a bell kept tolling in the background.

He awoke, sweating with fear. It was Sunday morning and the bell of his dreams was a church bell. *The Sabbath!* he thought, as he crept out of bed, shivering; the sky was clear, a single pane of blue edged with gold, the gold of the late year's sun. In the back court, two black trees had frost on their branches; he could not deny something of beauty in the scene. He turned and slipped back into bed, and lay there listening to the bells. Transported back through the years, he was holding his mother's hand as they followed behind his father, going down to the old church in Drumbeg. He remembered that Davie had given him the name of the church he attended; it was in one of his pockets. But he was surely crazy to be thinking like this? He had given up going to church; it reminded him too much of all that he had found repressive in his father's treatment of him. Still, he found himself crawling out of bed. He caught sight of himself in the single cracked mirror and noted the unkempt hair and unshaven chin. *There is no time* he told himself. The excuse relaxed him and he went back to bed once more. But he could not sleep. Damn it all! He got up again, shaved, and dressed in the best clothes he had. Outside, he began to run towards the sound of the bells. *Why on earth am I doing this?*, he asked himself as he ran; *I had decided never to go inside a church again. But I have to admit, I miss the psalms. It will be good to hear the psalms again.*

The singing had already begun when he slipped into the back pew, where an old lady whose whisper smelled of peppermint leaned across to show him the psalm. The swelling wave of strong voices rose and fell about him, a stern tide. Somewhere within, he thought, there is an anchor, made of a strong metal - if only I understood, if only I could find it. What was it that held my mother so surely, that my grandmother trusted in, aye, that gives that strength to Catriona as well? And yet in some strange way, even although he did not begin to understand, it seemed as though some strong invisible hand held him at that moment, a hand he did not fear.

'I to the hills will lift mine eyes.' That psalm above all! He looked up to the high beams of the roof as though somewhere in the plaster there was Beinn Dobhran. And he who had not believed for a long time, not truly since he was a child, found himself singing in a strong, clear voice. 'The moon by night thee shall not smite, nor yet the sun by day.' He had never been more conscious of his need; he felt as if he had at last found pure water amid the filth of the city; he drank in the words as he sang them, and felt cleansed and renewed. He watched in delight a little girl who sat with her mother near him; she swung her short legs backwards and forwards beneath the pew, and pointed things out to her mother in whispers - a twist of silver paper on the floor, a bird high on a branch outside. He saw those small things with her and did not think them foolish; they mattered to her, were part of her small world. They reminded him of the butterflies he had longed to reach at her age, the blooms he could not stretch high enough to pick. And he thought of experiments they did in his biology class; they would take a whole flower and dissect it, so that they could see the cells of the living organism. Yet there was no possibility of putting it together again, of restoring the loveliness that had been. And he wondered if that was what faith was like - seeing the whole, as it were, from afar, taking things on trust; for when one came too near with critical eyes, with eyes screwed up looking for proof, the picture was gone.

All these thoughts tumbled around in his mind as the light of the midday sun pierced through the windows and gilded the face of the minister as he leaned forward in the high pulpit. Dan realised with a start that he had listened to very little of the sermon. They were singing the final psalm; and suddenly he was again standing small between his father and mother in the church at home. Then he had longed to escape; the river and the woods were calling to him to come. Here, he had no desire to face all that lay outside. He decided to linger for a while in the warm church after the folk had gone. Then he caught sight of Davie far in front, just rising as the congregation began to go out. He rose and went out into the knife-sharp cold, realising all at once how hungry he was.

Chapter 11

It was more of an accident than anything else that Dan saved the little boy's life. All he saw was a momentary glimpse of small legs pumping; then he heard a woman's voice raised further away. As he crossed to the other side of the street, there was an impact as a small brown head dunted his thigh. It had all happened in an instant. Then the boy was lying on the ground, crying bitterly, and a young woman was bending quickly to pick him up and soothe him, while the elderly man in the motor who had had to jam on his brakes was shaking his fist angrily at the little party.

'I'm so sorry,' Dan said shyly to the boy's mother. She was quite a young girl, he noticed, who was cleaning her son's face with her handkerchief. She looked up sharply, saying simply:

'Sorry? But . . . you saved his life! He would have gone under that motor. I can't thank you enough.'

She smiled at Dan, who accepted dumbly what she had said. She was not in the least shy or embarrassed, he thought, and spoke as if he had been an old friend. She was capable too; she had the little boy calmed and smiling again, and looking up at Dan with interest, his face red and his eyes bright, the fright forgotten already.

'Well, I'm glad to have done something right for once,' Dan said laughing.

'How can I ever repay you?'. Her voice was serious but he heard the gratitude in her tone. 'Come with us, please, and have a cup of tea.'

It was a bitterly cold day. Dan's hands were red and sore with cold, the wind seeming to cut through him as he crossed between the tenements. He was feeling lonely as usual, not having spoken to anyone all day; yet he was shy of accepting the invitation. All the same he felt suddenly warmed and happy, and knew that he would go. He listened to the little boy's chatter as he now skipped at the end of his mother's hand. Dan stole a quick look at the girl; she was pretty, her face almost surrounded by dark-gold curls, eyes that were mischievous-looking, a very dark blue. Her son, he thought, was a small replica of her.

Over tea, they talked. He was glad of its warmth, holding his hands gratefully around the cup. She told him that she had a good job in an office, and worked there in the mornings while the boy went to his aunt's.

'And in the afternoons I am with Daniel,' she added.

'Dan?' he asked in surprise.

'Daniel,' the little boy answered firmly.

She caught Dan's glance and they both laughed. He noticed the dimples in her cheeks and he felt excited, happier than he had felt for a long time. He touched her arm as she looked out of the tearoom window and asked if she wanted more tea. She was doubtful about spending more time there but he persuaded her; it seemed important that they should go on talking. He did not ask about Daniel's father, but framed his questions carefully enough to know that he was not with them now. Her name was Susan Baird, she told him, and she and her son lived in a small flat left her by her parents, who had both died young. Daniel was four. She ruffled his hair lovingly as she spoke, and he got up on the seat and stretched up to be hugged. There was something sad in her, Dan thought, but she was beautiful! He thought that if he were an artist he would want to paint her here, sitting in the corner of the cheap restaurant, the people coming in with their coats buttoned against the early December cold. But he could only paint the picture in the recesses of his mind; and for a second it seemed to him that she had a look of his mother.

He walked home with them, even though he had been on his way to the library and it was in the other direction. Before they left the main street he dived into a shop and reappeared with a bar of chocolate for Daniel. She seemed more pleased than the boy, but it did not matter. He found himself telling Susan all about his course, how lazy he had been from the beginning, how strange it still was to him; she said he was like all other students, spoiled and a bit mad. But her eyes teased when she said it, and they both laughed again. It was so easy to laugh with her, he could hardly remember when he had last found so many things amusing. They reached the bottom of the stone steps leading up to her flat, and Daniel went running up ahead.

'Can I see you again?' Dan asked shyly, suddenly a boy again.

She had started up the stairs but now looked round, and was quiet for a moment.

'You know where we live. I can't stop you.' She went up a few more steps and then turned again and said in a warmer tone:

'Yes, come back; I'd like you to. Daniel and I see very few folk.'

Dan went back to his cheerless room with a deep glow of happiness in him; and he worked hard that night. Catriona was a broken image at the back of his mind but tonight he hardly cared; he told himself that loneliness was destroying him; he just had to have companionship. He had been alone too long already.

But he did not go back for a few days, until the Christmas vacation had begun. He was not going home, but had been to the station and witnessed fifty farewells as his fellow students had departed for their homes. He had gone to all of his term exams, but had not done well. He knew he had not deserved to; he had skimped on his work. Now he could not wait to see Susan and Daniel again. He went back, was welcomed by them both and felt a warmth he had almost forgotten; soon he was on his way to see them at every chance, and as he had poured out affection on his mother, so he began to do now on them both. When he could get hold of a piece of wood he delighted himself in carving, bringing rough-cut squirrels and bears out of it for the little boy. Susan, he soon found, had been used to men who treated her hard; she had known little tenderness at all since her parents had died. She gave herself to Dan because she trusted him, realising that to him this was no game; he was simple Dan, swinging at times between sorrow and a boy's laughter, sincere and vulnerable. They came together because each had known much of suffering; they saw understanding and compassion in each other's eyes.

For the first time in his life, Dan celebrated Christmas; only New Year had been recognised in the glen. They had a festive dinner of chicken and plum pudding, and in addition a tiny tree with tinsel, and crackers and balloons, both a novelty to Dan. Susan laughed and said he was more of a child than Daniel.

At New Year, a parcel came from Catriona. He did not want to open it; he felt sick with betrayal. She had packed little gifts for him - her own cake, a bag of hazel nuts she had picked in the autumn, a pair of warm gloves knitted by herself, even his favourite treacle toffee. From his father there were socks and handkerchiefs. Everything he touched burned him; he felt wretched and hollow and found himself wishing there had been silence instead; it was all he deserved. Or at least, some kind of reprimand in the note that came with the gifts. But there was nothing but kindness and acceptance. He quickly sent back presents for the two of them, with a card but no letter, but his feelings of guilt were in no way assuaged. He did not allow himself to think of the glen, of Achnagreine, when the turn of the year came, and he did not even go to Susan. Despising himself, he turned instead to the whisky bottle and a brief easing of his pain.

Soon, though, he was back at the little flat with small gifts for mother and son. His need of love, he realised, was greater than Susan's. She had steered her life cold and bitter since her small son's birth, content to pour her love into him; men had betrayed her and she had lost her faith. Dan needed her to be there, to hold him and comfort him. She was at least a substitute for all he had once known, and represented home now that home was gone.

The old man came out of the tight enclosure of the wood and was now standing in snow - a long ridge that had been blown by the spring gales and had not as yet receded to show the green alive underneath. He was impatient now to be away from the trees, to stand free on the open moor land. The lochans were above him, in the long saddle that lay beneath the jagged neck of Beinn Dobhran. They reminded him of blue brooches, pinned to the deep heather plaid that was spread all around. He would not reach them today and he shivered as the fear came to him that he might never see them again. Had he indeed come up here to say farewell? There arose in him a dark panic like the wings of many birds, and he felt his heart flutter against his chest. Oh, for the chance to wind time back and stand here a boy again, his breath strong and his feet ready for many miles ahead! Such days were gone; the tree he now was stood grey and bent and almost broken. A tree must be cut down, though, for the seedlings to grow; but roots, surely the roots may remain for ever, to be discovered by succeeding generations of workers who tend the land. He did not want this place to forget him.

Many a time Dan had fancied that his spirit would linger here after his death. Was that mere wishful thinking? To see the lochs with the evening breeze just right for a cast, the snow as it came over the moors almost horizontal on the wind's knife, the merlins, the soaring of eagles in a clear sky. As a boy he had had the same fearful thoughts of death, the same terror lest all he loved in this glen were to be blacked out in a single moment; but then he had tried to imagine what it would be like to live to be eighty, and had decided that if that time ever came he would be content to say goodbye. Here he was now, having come so far; yet there was not a part of his spirit that did not cry out against the sadness of leaving this land behind. Despite his faith, despite his longing to see again those whom he had loved in life, this was still the truth.

He sat down painfully between two boulders of quartz and held his hands between his knees, for they were very cold. He listened to the curlews as they rose up from beneath him - what more lovely cry was there in all the world? This was the very edge of the cultivated land; he felt that beyond here nothing had been touched or changed since the beginning of time. It was intact, a kind of reconstruction of creation. Now they talked of coming here to make a dam, to flood the upper part of the corrie here to generate power - how long had it been since he had heard Kate mention it? He could not remember, and in any case he could not fight them; they would not listen. They wanted jobs and money and fast lives. Everything was changing. He did not even want to keep up. At least most of Achnagreine was still safe, though the men who had bought the land round the Lodge had put up a deer fence, a shining metal wall that seemed to leer at him when he caught sight of it from the window on the stairs. Was it set up to keep him out?

It was no good, he was tired of thinking of all the changes, all the threats of the modern age. His thoughts returned once more to that far-away time in Glasgow; as he sat in the lee of the boulders, the years he had lost came back to him in vivid detail. What he had thrown away, to gain nothing in return! Or perhaps he *had* found something - in that each day of his years of captivity had as it were prepared the soil of his heart for the harvest that would come later. Never again would he be in any doubt about the things that were important to him.

He had not remained at university beyond a year. By then he had made more than enough enemies among the staff; at first encouraging, tolerant of his excuses for work not done, they had in the end lost patience with him. At the start of the summer term, as his relationship with Susan had grown more intense, he had taken to staying later and later at her flat most nights; things had deteriorated from then on, the gaps between his attendances at the rooms in the quadrangles growing ever greater. Dan even now in his old age could recall clearly how he used to creep downstairs like a mouse in the small hours - Susan was scared lest any of her highly respectable neighbours should complain. He reflected wryly how things had changed; today he might have moved in with Susan and not an eyebrow would have been raised.

But as he thought over the reasons for his leaving, he knew it had not simply been due to the neglect of his studies but, more profoundly, to his conscious rejection of much of the teaching offered; more especially, of the way in which it was carried out. He had become aware that not enough freedom was given to students to argue their own case and his growing convictions were being stifled. Above all he wanted to be allowed to think for himself; yet it appeared useless to attempt to deviate from his tutors' line of thinking.

'I feel the claustrophobia of it all in the very walls,' he remembered saying dramatically to MacKenzie, his philosophy tutor, on the day when he had finally come to the conclusion that it was useless for him to continue.

'Maybe it's a fault in myself,' he had gone on, 'but I never imagined I'd be prevented from thinking for myself. It is as if there is always a choice of answers that have been worked out before, and all I am expected to do is to pick one out, like a parrot. Yet I'm sure we have to go on searching for answers! We can't just stop - we go on and on because there are always doubts and always discoveries.'

How surprised he had been at himself for daring to 'talk back' to a lecturer in this way, remembering how he had looked up at the dark high tower that seemed to stretch up to the sky, reminding him of the Tower of Babel.

'But you simply must go on,' MacKenzie had replied, exasperation showing in his face and voice. 'You have to get over this first stage and then go on into research - the whole world can open up for you then and people will listen to you because you have proved yourself. Undergraduates often feel as you do - the best ones too. Yes, I include you,' he added, almost smiling.

'All these years lost in the city,' Dan had murmured half to himself.

MacKenzie had sighed and let him go. Dan knew he thought him strange; he did not care.

After days of searching, he found a job. It was the last thing he wanted, in a stuffy office five floors up, endlessly filing letters and papers and checking mail; but his money was fast running out, and he was fully aware that he was lucky to have a job at all, in this city of mass unemployment, poverty and degradation. He turned his eyes the other way as he passed the lines of miserable-looking men at the 'buroo'. He told himself constantly that he ought to be thankful, yet he felt the work drowned his spirit. The office looked down on a school playground, and he saw that the children had nothing but concrete and high railings - no grass, no trees, nowhere to run and be free. Somehow he envied them, as he did the butterflies he set free from the window all that interminable summer. He felt crushed. Life had become a treadmill of days to be gone through; trams to his work and back again, miles and miles of dingy streets that seemed to have no end.

His room saw less and less of him as on most evenings he almost ran to Susan's flat. It seemed to him that she breathed on him and the pieces of his shattered self were put together again. He tried to appear strong and buoyant in her presence, fearing above all things that she would look down on him because he was several years younger, still perhaps in her eyes a boy; but in the end he would always break. She was the only solace he knew, in among this seeming maze of concrete and stone, dirt and despair. Daniel too provided balm to his spirit. He took him to the park and pushed him on his favourite swing; the little boy's delighted laughter gave him joy. There were cats to stroke on the way home, raindrops hanging from railings to touch, games of hide and seek to play. Above all he took delight in telling Daniel what life in the country was like. The child never tired of that.

'Tell me more 'bout the glen,' he would beg Dan.

Dan needed no urging. He spent hours describing the farm with its animals, fishing in the river, the woods. Once Susan said quite sharply that he must stop putting ideas in the boy's head. Later, they quarrelled about it; she told him her grandfather had been a sheep farmer in Argyll and had had to come to Glasgow, penniless, after he had lost everything. Daniel probably had farming in his blood, she said, but she did not want that for him. She did not want him to end up penniless. Dan argued back furiously, pleading with her to come to the country with him and let Daniel be happy. She ruffled his hair and shook her head.

'Your head is in the clouds, Dan. There are no roads to your places. You'll see one day when you've gone as far as I have.'

That was by no means their only quarrel. As time went on, Dan began to have deep doubts about their relationship. He asked himself *Have I stopped loving her? Have I ever really loved her? Is it love or simply infatuation? Or is it only that I need a mother?*

Even in Susan's embrace, he would sometimes see Catriona's face. He had tried to bury that memory because of the sense of guilt and betrayal it brought. In his waking hours he usually managed to suppress it; in dreams he was beaten. Again and again he dreamed of his mother; sometimes he would be following her, and then she would turn round, and the face would be Catriona's. When his birthday came, she sent him a cake with twenty candles. He could hardly bear to look at it. He could not write in thanks because he had no idea what he could say.

Back with Susan again, he saw the hurt that lay in her as deep as knife-wounds. Men had abused her; Daniel's father had walked out on her when he found she was pregnant; she had had to fight hard to keep her son and bring him up by herself. Dan recognised the hardness she had been forced to grow as a shell around her; she looked out from the battlements of her world and let only Daniel inhabit that imprisoned place. He saw that he did not know her, that she would never allow him to know her. He could come no closer. They were on guard with each other.

One Saturday he went down to the Clyde. Almost a year had gone by since he had left his studies but he felt much more than a year older. He did not give up his job because times were hard, and he helped Susan a little and barely managed to make ends meet. Now he sometimes found himself envying the students he saw, wishing he could begin again. Today he walked through mean streets he had never seen before. Wherever he looked there was poverty. He kicked a bottle by mistake and it spun round on the pavement; some people arguing at the mouth of a close turned and shouted obscenities at him. A woman was crying inside one of the tenements he passed; he seemed to hear her for a very long time, and her crying seemed to embody all the misery he saw around him. He had a sense of fear; there was a thin mist hanging over the city like a spider's web; it got into one's hair and the back of one's throat. He stood there at last looking at the yards where the great ships were built. He knew that many of them were silent now, with huge numbers of men out of work. He watched the water, dead and still like a huge pane of glass, the cranes leaning over the river like herons watching for fish. But any fish were long gone from here. The water was dead, poisoned; nothing could survive there.

He began to think about Susan. He could see her in his mind as she would be now, getting the supper ready, talking to Daniel, answering his questions. And he realised with a sense of shock that he had run away; he had come here because he no longer wanted to be with her. He listened to the long, low hooting of a tug as it turned and went west into the fading light. Then he began to retrace his steps. But after a short time he knew he had gone wrong; he had no recollection of having taken this way before. In the middle of a wide street with derelict tenements on either side, he saw a gang of youths standing; one of them held a bottle in his hand. He turned quickly and went down a narrow lane; a dog leapt out at him, snarling; a man dragged it away with a curse. An old crippled woman appeared on the other side; Dan started to cross to ask directions, but stopped, fearing she might be afraid of him. He passed a derelict station and, looking through the broken walls that echoed at his approach, remembered the day - so long ago it seemed - when he had first arrived in the city and had looked north to the end of the tunnel. He suddenly saw himself walking on the railway track, mile after mile, the only sure way of reaching home. He felt as if he had awakened from a long sleep, only the nightmare from which he had thought to escape from was reality. He found himself trembling all over. He was in a place from which there was no escape! He began to walk blindly; let him at all costs get away from here. He tripped on something and bent to pick it up. To his surprise he found it was part of a branch; probably some child had snapped it from a tree. Even in the sickly light he could still see the green edge beneath the bark. Suddenly the picture of his father cutting down the old rowan came back to him in vivid detail, the branches being sawn, the bunches of red berries. The thought of the glen became very real to him; and with it came a faint sense of hope. Maybe there would yet be a way back.

A few days later he had the dream. It was after he had had another row with Susan; he had reprimanded Daniel for swearing and she had shouted at him that this was her child and she would tell him how to behave. He accused her of shutting him out; she retorted that he was like every other man she had known - they all wanted women as possessions to hold and control. He said quietly that he only wanted to love her but she was too proud and bitter to accept love. She turned and left the room, banging the door. Not knowing what else to do, he had gone back to his lonely room.

Misery came over him like a cloud. He felt the old fear once more, the fear that he was trapped in this place for ever. If he should die without every seeing the glen again! That meant more to him than seeing any human being, he thought. But there was Catriona - what if he should never see her again? What if she had gone, left Achnagreine, without saying where she was going? He must go home; he must! He knelt by the window with his head in his hands; then darkness came and he lit his lamp, and got out the bottle of whisky and a glass. He drank until his eyes swam, and then he went to bed and slept.

In the dream a man came into his room and led him away, down the stone stairs in his bare feet, through places where he had never been before, until he was utterly exhausted and lost. But they came to the River Clyde and followed it, back out of Glasgow and then away up into a valley and the open country beyond. Dan felt his feet torn on sharp stones but the man who led him never once slackened his pace, until they came to a place where the river was a white waterfall, deep and narrow. He lifted his eyes and saw, far away on the north side, Achnagreine and the hills. He wanted to rush down the last few steps to cross the river, but realised it would be useless for he would be swept away by the strong current. As he turned helplessly to his guide, he saw two tall trees on the near side; both were covered with red berries. The man had an axe in his hand; he approached the trees.

'Don't cut them! Don't cut them!' Dan heard himself crying, though his feet were rooted to the spot and he could go no nearer. He was filled with fear because he knew the trees were rowans.

'Do you not want to cross?' answered the man in a deep voice. 'Then we must cut the trees to build a bridge.' The axe flashed in the air; the strokes fell, regular as the seconds of a clock.

With a start he awoke; the clock in the hall was chiming: one, two, three, four. Sweating with fear, he lay for a few moments and then got up, wincing at the thud of pain in his head.

He knew from that moment, without the slightest doubt, that today he was going home. The certainty was so total, so absolutely clear, that he asked himself almost in wonder why he had not gone before. *It was because of my father,* he answered himself; *I was afraid of him.* But why? *Because I thought he would be angry at my failure in my studies; and more - I was afraid he would gain some kind of power over me when I came crawling back in failure and shame.* And if he *is* angry, if he refuses to accept me? *Then I'll find work somewhere else in the glen, and at least I'll be there - and maybe, just maybe, there will be Catriona as well, and she'll forgive me.* His heart leapt as he began to take it all in; the river was crossed, he was going home!

But first there were things to be done. He determined to leave this place in debt to no-one. With trembling hands he carefully counted out his money. Yes, he had enough. Enough for his fare and a bit more, once he had left two weeks' money for his landlady - the rent he owed, plus an extra week's rent in lieu of notice. That was the agreement. He wrote her a note. Then he wrote a letter of resignation from his job. *Nothing could give me greater pleasure,* he thought; *what a waste of all those days!* Here, too, he would have to forfeit a week's wages through leaving without notice. What did it matter? On impulse he added a fervent plea that his job might be given to a friend and neighbour, desperate for a job; he enclosed their address.

Just one thing more. He must write to Susan. That was more difficult; but he knew she would not grieve at his going. More likely she would be relieved. Daniel would cry for him, and as he wrote, tears were in his own eyes for the little boy who had given him so much. In a parcel he packed for him the only things he had to leave him - the cows and sheep and terracotta barns of the toy farm, the present his brother Andrew had given him as he left for France. He hoped fervently that one day Daniel would indeed find his way to the country and become a farmer like his grandfather, although sadly it seemed unlikely.

Then he turned to his own packing. He found room for everything in his two battered cases, left his room spotless, and shut the door behind him. It was still early; he saw no-one as he let himself out. He went to the Post Office, which had just opened, and posted the parcel. He then walked to the station, and waited for the first train to Abercree.

Chapter 12

Going north on that morning train Dan seemed to be the only one awake. It was not quite light yet and Glasgow lay shrouded in a yellowish fog. Just a frail light here and there in the tenement windows as the train went slowly past. Dan said a thankful 'goodbye' to the city - to every empty window and street and back-court; he could hardly contain his joy at the thought that he would not be coming back. As though a war had ended and the wounded were on their way home - that was how it appeared to him as he sat looking across at the sleeping faces of his fellow travellers opposite.

Then it was over, the houses left behind. To the north lay the fields and low hills. A sharp ray of sun bled from the east, red and strong, like the single string of a great harp; he closed his eyes and felt the warm light on his face. Now he slept, relaxed and dreamless, as a child might have done. So he returned to Abercree, impatience surging in him as he got out on to the familiar platform. So nearly home, and still not there! Once more he carefully counted out his remaining coins. He had just enough to buy a small twist of tobacco for his father and some chocolates for Catriona - please, please let her be there! Then he met a farmer from up the glen who offered him a lift home in his old Morris; gratefully Dan climbed in with his heavy cases. He answered the man's questions as briefly as was possible; he did not want to talk; there was so much to drink in, and he was half-mad with joy. It was as autumn had always been! The edges of blue sky blown by the wind, the leaves coming like red-gold wings from the trees, the river sparkling with sharp light. He felt as if each place was nodding to him, welcoming him on his return. He watched on one side and then on the other, delirious with happiness. And after they had passed Drumbeg, he plucked up the courage to say to his benefactor that if he didn't mind, he would get out a mile or so before Achnagreine, as he wanted to walk the last bit.

'You'll think me daft, I know,' he added apologetically.

The man did not seem to mind, and added kindly that he would leave Dan's cases at the foot of the brae for him. He drove away, Dan shouting his thanks. And then he was walking, alone, looking up at the Beinn above him edged with just a breath of mist, the slopes russet with bracken. On impulse he leapt over a fence into a field where a chestnut tree grew; how good it was to see one again! Would there be conkers? He could hardly contain his laughter as he shuffled among the fallen leaves, stuffing the polished nuts into his pockets. *I'll never grow up*, he told himself; *they'll always give me a thrill.*

Quieter now, he reached the final stretch. He saw the churchyard and stopped, at first irresolute. Then he went in, his feet noiseless on the wet ground. His heart beating fast, he went round and found his mother's grave, saw the stone with her name on it:

Rena Maclean, beloved wife of John Drummond

Incised at the foot, the familiar words from Revelation - *Gus am bris an latha* - 'until the day breaks'. He bent down close to the stone, and whispered:

'I've come back, mother; and I'll never leave again.'

His eyes burned, but this time there was no deep grief, rather a feeling of peace.

He stood and listened. A robin was singing - the sound of autumn. There were autumn smells too; how well he remembered them! All the years seemed to flood into one, all the impressions and memories that made the rich tapestry of his past life in this place. He heard the river going over its rugged bed. The waterfalls are past, he thought; he had climbed back from the sea to the fresh water, the only stream that could satisfy his thirst. And his mother was in all that grew so richly in this place; she was in all the beauty he loved, which she had taught him to love. He would grieve no more for her now.

Soon he had reached the last part and his heart thundered. Who did he want to meet first at Achnagreine? For the hundredth time he wondered if Catriona would be there, and if she was, would she welcome him? But he had to meet his father first. He had no idea what he would do, what he would say. There had been a betrayal, he knew that; it had happened, and it had as it were purified his blood. Now his need of journeying was over, and his father must know that. The long, cold war was over as well; the old juvenile pride had stopped eating at him. A mother and a wife was gone; father and son must surely bear the grief together.

He saw the heavy cases where they had been left at the foot of the brae leading up to the farm but he left them lying. He wanted to run the last bit, to drive straight into that knot of fear inside, to summon up all his strength. He was in bad condition, he realised as he came to the crest of the hill; in the old days he could have run twenty times farther and not noticed. None of the dogs was about, so his father did not turn round from the place where he was crouching at the far side, the burn side, of the yard, mixing some paint. Dan went slowly and stood there, seeing the bent back and grey head. The sun came suddenly from behind him and his shadow was cast dark on the wall. His father turned, then said just one word.

'Dan!'

Then he felt his eyes swim helplessly and he put his arms round his father and was half-laughing, half-crying; as though a sac of poison had burst inside him, he felt bonds released and the clenched fist of his bitterness relaxed at long last. It no longer mattered what his father thought now. He had as it were thrown himself across the wide gulf that had been between them with a whole heart; he had beaten swords into ploughshares. He was back where his heart belonged. And when he looked again at his father, he was smiling with a joy he never remembered seeing on his face before. He was an altogether older man now, Dan realised, older and more

111

weary; the lines in his face, like the rings of a tree, spoke of suffering. But he was still who he had always been, his father, proud and determined. Dan, still holding on to him, found himself muttering:

'The prodigal, father . . . forgive me.'

Johnny was unable to answer. Dan saw that he was fighting to control himself; he just shook his head and, half-choking, said:

'Thank God.'

'Well, no doubt we'll hear all your news in due course,' he finally managed in a more normal voice.

Dan, turning away towards the house, could not help smiling to himself; it might have been that he had been away for a weekend! *It won't have seemed the eternity to him that it has to me*, he thought.

But his father amazed him by adding in a quiet voice: 'Two years and thirty-one days - it's been a long time, son.'

Dan stopped in his tracks, and for a long moment they just looked at each other.

Then his father, smiling again, said 'Away in then and see Catriona. It's herself will be glad to see you.'

He spoke to him as a boy still, but for once Dan didn't mind; he went swiftly to the kitchen door and opened it wide, stepped over the dogs and stood there, looking at Catriona as she sat at the kitchen table. She looked up, frowning a little as if the light was bad and she was not sure who it was. Scared, uncertain of what to say, Dan found himself adopting a loud, falsely hearty tone.

'Oh, come on, Catriona, surely you can do better than that!' he said, forcing a cheery grin.

He went towards her and then stopped, his smile falling away under the simplicity of her gaze. He felt naked, her eyes boring into his very soul. She said nothing. Then she got up and, calm as anything, walked slowly over to the fire. He felt his heart quaking.

'Catriona! Don't keep me in suspense!' he begged. 'At least speak to me, after all this time.'

Now her eyes flashed at him. 'Aye, Dan, after all this time, indeed! Is it any wonder when you go off and forget folk's very existence? Do you really expect me to throw my arms round your neck and say it's all fine, after what you did to us?'

Her voice rose in anger and she leaned forward, firing her words at him like gunfire.

'Do you have any idea how I waited, Dan? How I wondered every day for two whole years if there would be some word from you, just one word even? And there was nothing - month after month of nothing. And I had really believed you cared.'

Her voice broke and she hid her face from him, crying like a child. She slumped into a chair and covered her face with her hands. And then he was down on his knees beside her, wretched with the deep guilt he felt; he put his arms round her, kissed her hair and her face and hands, stroked his fingers through the beautiful soft hair.

'I know, I know,' he whispered brokenly. 'I hate myself, Catriona - you'll never know how much I hate and despise myself. I never knew . . . never meant . . . I could never be sure if you could love me. But that's why I did come back in the end. I went wrong . . . I'm not worthy of you, wouldn't deserve you in a hundred years. But I didn't forget you ever; I swear I didn't!'

She turned to him then and said simply:

'Hold me, Dan, and don't go away - don't *ever* go away again!'

It was all he could have asked for, far more than he deserved; and he closed his eyes, smelled the warm fragrance of her hair, touched the soft skin of her cheek. They comforted each other and he felt he was offering her his whole heart, swearing never to betray her again. He would have liked to confess all that he had done, to gain peace of mind; but he knew that would have been to buy his peace at the expense of hers. Then a glow of absolute happiness spread through him; it came to him that only that morning he had been in Glasgow and he had had nothing. Now his hands were filled with a harvest richer than any lord's. Knowing he did not deserve any of it, he felt gratitude well up in him. In the end it was Catriona who pressed him away from her, smiling.

'This won't do, Dan,' she said. 'I've got to make your father's tea - and yours'.

He nodded. 'There's something I have to do anyway,' he answered. 'Don't worry - I'll be back in time. I could eat an elephant'.

He kissed her and went out of the kitchen into the yard, beginning to run. He passed his father but did not stop until he came to the burn. There was still plenty of time, he thought. Up and up the steep sides of the burn he clambered until his breath was coming fast. But it felt good! The blood sang in his ears and there was a cool breeze in his face. Once he tripped on bracken and fell headlong, but he only rolled over, panting and laughing, and then drove himself on mercilessly straight up the steep slope until it levelled out and there were birches and he could see the white tail of the falls. How long was it since he had been here last? This most special place - the place his mother had always loved best for a picnic, the last place they had been together. For a moment he paused, panting; there were ghosts in this place and he could not but be aware of them. He went down slowly then to the wide black ring of the pool. Donnie's Pool. There was still a smudged edge of sun coming from the west, shining in a golden bell on the water's surface. It was mad, he thought, what he wanted to do, but he was going to do it. He threw off his clothes and stood for a moment, shivering, looking at himself in the mirror of the water. He was thinner, he knew, much thinner than he had been when he left; and he felt his face had changed in some way. Then with a great yell he plunged into the deep black pool and he was gasping and blowing, wildly waving his arms and ducking his head under the freezing water. His whole body ached with cold, but he scrubbed his face and hands and dived back under the water and opened his eyes to the pain of the cold. Only then did he stumble back out, gushing streams of water.

Later, dried and warmed after a run around the bank, he sat for a few moments of reflection. He was clean again, the city dirt washed away. Healed, too - at least in part. It would take a long time before he forgave himself, he knew. He thought of the sincerity with which his father had breathed the words 'Thank God'. What about him? Could he believe in this God who was so real to his father - and Catriona? He had found himself thinking of himself as the prodigal returning; I could almost recite the whole story after all these years, he thought; my mother taught it to me so thoroughly. Can I really be forgiven, just like that? Half-embarrassed, he muttered a prayer.

'God, if you're there, forgive me. Guide me from now on. And . . . thanks. For everything.'

He got up and ran down to the house.

Chapter 13

Dan came back down from the moor, Beinn Dobhran like a dark hand guiding his left shoulder. He had wanted to climb higher, but he simply had not the strength in him. The streams chuckled as he crossed them; for a moment his shadow would fall on them, then he was forgotten. Compared with them, he thought, he was a mere child! What was he in time but the quickest blink of the eyes, the fall of a stone? Yet in his mind his life had been a long time, many hard miles of marching.

He would skirt the wood now, come down over the moorland and the lion grass - as his mother had always called it - to the cave, the place of shelter. It was hidden among the rocks, so that many would fail to find it; but not he - he could find it blindfolded. But as he walked on, the keen wind came sharp across his face and a thin mist blew over, covering like a fleece the hollow between Beinn Dobhran and the Tor up to his right. The whole wood was swallowed up and the glen vanished. The breeze was edged with a smirr of rain like tiny pearls that clung to his face and neck. The ground was thick with boggy hollows, and there were but few stones to use as footholds. Often Dan had to stop, precariously balanced, spying out as a hawk might the next place of landing. He kept going right, towards the piled rocks at the base of the Tor where the cave was, but it seemed much further than before. His chest had begun to hurt, and he was forced to stop, wheezing, bent on one knee on a gnarled lump of quartz, angry with himself for his weakness.

Now he felt an edge of fear cutting at his mind - what if he had gone wrong, disorientated by the mist? Surely not! It wounded him even to think that might happen to him, of all people. But he should have been over this ground long ago! Then, without warning, like an owl rising, the mist cleared and he was free, and the glen lay below him bathed in fresh light the colour of golden corn.

Even then, he did not at first find his way to the cave. He could not be sure whether it was above Spies' Rock or not. In the end he blundered across it, finding the low entrance sodden with water; two sheep which had been lying near rose on thin legs and ran away. He saw that they were slow and heavy with their lambs.

Shivering, he decided to stay in the cave for a brief rest and get warm again. Thankfully he crouched there in the semi-darkness, looking around and noting the corner in which his father had found flints and potsherds which had later been found to be of great antiquity. Memories connected with this cave flooded back as he sat there; but he had not yet reached that part of his life, he was not ready to retrace those particular steps. Instead, he began to recall the chapter which had followed his return from Glasgow.

He and Catriona had been married the following summer. At least, he thought wryly, it had put an end to the glen gossip that had driven the two of them mad and which had begun even before he had left for the city. After Glasgow, though, whenever he was tempted to lose patience with the old women who seemed to be forever whispering when they came out of church, he would force himself to remember the frightening anonymity of the city, and tell himself to be thankful for the identity he had here. Folk were simply interested; but it was no good, it still annoyed him! An old lady for whom he was working once asked him how his father was coping with the drought. He had answered that it was a bother getting water from the spring, but that he and Catriona helped. At this the old lady's eyes lit up - like a crocodile's, Dan thought to himself maliciously - and she put down her cup with a clatter.

'Now Dan,' she said eagerly, 'maybe you can put us right about this. They're saying that you and Catriona . . . that you're going together. Is that true?'

There was a moment of silence as she leaned forward expectantly. He couldn't resist it - he was half raging, half laughing inside as he calmly replied.

'Well, some say we are, and some say we're not; you just don't know who to believe sometimes, do you?'

He went home whistling, feeling that a score had been settled.

In any case he married Catriona. It wasn't many weeks after he had asked her that they had the wedding down at Drumbeg. The day they got engaged, he remembered, his father insisted Catriona must go home for a month's holiday, until the wedding; it would not be right for them to be in the same house. Nothing ever changed in the glen, he had thought at the time. Some sixty years before, his grandmother Eliza had been found lodgings with the gamekeeper's family until her marriage with Alan could take place; here was the same thing happening again! They missed Catriona, and fully realised how much unseen work she did, during those weeks of absence.

His father cleared one of the barns, and the wedding ceilidh went on until it was morning and the hills were shaded with August light. Dan remembered with absolute clarity the picture of old Jean Cameron being whirled round so fast in 'Strip the Willow' that she was nearly sent through the wall without an arm. But what he remembered best was Catriona, his beautiful bride. There had been no honeymoon for them; Dan was starting work on the following Monday repairing a drystone dyke for an old man down the glen. Nor did they feel the slightest need to go away. And why should they? They had each other, and everything else they could possibly want or need, at the farm. There was the beauty of the hills all around, and more than enough work to be done. They had a room and a bed to share and took delight in each other. All these years later, Dan's pulse still quickened as he recalled the richness of those far-away days. It was as if they came tumbling one after another like clear water from a well. Never had he known such absolute joy, such deep contentment which filled his whole being.

He worked with his father for a while after his return, but the place simply was not big enough for them both. While before this had been because of the antagonism between them, now it was a simple fact. Dan would have to find other work. Finally he announced that he wanted training in fencing and dyking; since he had at last bought an old and battered Ford van, he could take work wherever he found it in the glen. So it came about that he was usually away for about three days each week; the extra money was welcomed by all three of them. Dan remembered how he had watched his father carefully at that time, to see whether, and in what ways, he had changed. Certainly much of the old hardness had gone since his wife's death, but he could still be stubborn and at times stern. He still appeared to be chained hopelessly to those few rough acres of land, and it was still almost reluctantly that he showed his care for Dan and Catriona; but both knew that strong feelings ran deep underneath. Sometimes Dan felt his father had become weaker, that he had not the same power either in hands or voice. He moved more heavily and became frustrated when his back pained him, but now there was no anger, no sign of rage or blame directed at either of them, just a silent sadness of which they could not but be aware. Now and then Dan would mention his mother, because he was conscious often of her nearness and wanted her to be kept alive among them. However, Johnny would not join in the talk; it was obvious that it caused him discomfort. His silent sadness was only too apparent to both Dan and Catriona, but nobody could doubt for a moment that he was still master of Achnagreine. Not once did it seem to have occurred to him to allow Dan to take over the farm now that he was married and settled; he clung, in a way almost pitifully, to all he owned there. Dan could never really imagine a time when the land would truly be his own.

All the same, Dan looked back on those early years of his marriage as a time when his world had never been so good. All of his happiness was built round his deep love for Catriona, and with his father too, there was a kind of peace as they sat by the fire together in the evenings after a hard day's work, listening to the wireless. This was a novelty they now shared with most of the glen folk - one which (apart from the nuisance of having to charge the batteries) on the whole had brought them much pleasure. It had brought in something of the outside world, and marked the beginning of many a change in the lives of the people.

One thing which it did bring in a very real way, and one which Dan could still remember all these years later with a sinking of the heart, was the fear of war. How well he still recalled the three of them sitting one night listening to the ravings of Hitler and the frightening roars of the Nuremberg crowds. They said little to each other; but Dan knew that all had experienced a kind of shattering of their peace.

The coming of war. When it came to thinking of this phase of his past life, Dan knew he was reluctant to re-move the covers; the pain was buried - let it remain so. But no, he had set himself the specific task of retracing all of his steps; he must face this too. So he began to re-live those days.

What he recalled most vividly - and with the most pain - were the sleepless nights. Nights when he had lain awake, Catriona asleep by his side, thrashing out, over and over again, his confused thoughts about this war. He knew he hated war with every fibre of his being. He hated violence - to man and beast, and it was something he knew he shared with his brother Andrew, the brother he had scarcely known at all, the brother who, hating to kill even a rabbit, had yet gone off to the hell of the trenches of the earlier war, and never returned. And this war? How could he go, leaving Catriona and his father, perhaps never to return either? But how could he not go? The very thought of Fascism and all it stood for was anathema to him. He would have to go. So he reasoned, as the long hours of the nights ticked by on the old clock by his bedside. At other times he decided that he was really a conscientious objector. But how could he be? He was too much of a coward, he decided, to follow that path - nobody in the glen would understand; he simply didn't have the courage. In any case, others were having to go, so why not himself? Iain and Dougie, his two best friends from schooldays, were already in the Air Force. Soon his own call-up papers would arrive. If it must be, he knew he would go.

But the weeks went by and no papers came. He was puzzled, especially when two school friends of his own age were called up. Then one day, a strange thing happened. Dan had been out on a dyking job and had gone home early, soaked to the skin. He had gone up to his room to change his wet clothes when he heard the doorbell - an unusual event, since neighbours were in the habit of simply walking into the kitchen. Then he heard voices raised in anger. His curiosity aroused, he pulled on a pair of dry trousers and in his bare feet went down the stairs and stood at the bottom, looking into the kitchen. Catriona was standing motionless by the stove, while his father faced a burly man in uniform who was clearly extremely irate.

'For God's sake, Drummond!' he was shouting, and Dan heard at once the alien English timbre in his voice. 'Surely you didn't think you'd get away with this?'

It was the sight of his father particularly that Dan would never forget. Drawn up to his full height, and seeming to tower over the other man, his face was deathly pale, his eyes blazing with a mixture of anger and distress.

'You tried to take away my land.'

It was as though he did not address this Englishman at all, but someone else, through and beyond him. His voice was deadly quiet and steady.

'You took away my first son,' he continued 'and he never came back. What did he have to die for? And you took away half of myself. Now you're asking for my other son and . . .,' his face becoming a spasm of fierce pride and anger, his huge hands knotted white and ugly

121

at his sides, 'and, if you do that, you'll kill a man, and his wife, and his father.'

Dan began now to step forward; it suddenly dawned on him that it was *his* life they were speaking of. *This is ludicrous*, he thought.

'I ask you again. Did you receive call-up papers?' the man in his correct English voice snapped at Dan.

'I told you!' Johnny seemed to fill the whole doorway with his rage. 'I kept them. I burned them!'

Then, turning to Dan, he shouted in a voice of sheer desperation.

'Dan! Listen! Listen, for all our sakes! Get out of here! Do what George did! Up to Beinn Dobhran and the hills, where they'll never find you!'

Dan met his father's pleading eyes, saw the white, rigid face of the military man, and felt Catriona at his elbow, close and pale the oval of her face.

For a moment as in a dream he saw himself in the snow. At the cave on the face of the hill, cutting from the bare rock the very bones of life. Coming down to the house to snatch in secrecy food, and Catriona's embrace; an exile from his own home. It was not right; it was not right. He was shaking his head at his father, then broke away suddenly from Catriona's arms.

'It's no good, father. You've fought them as far as you could, but no farther. I don't want to go either - Catriona, yourself, the glen.'

He looked back at Catriona for a moment and saw the bare white struggling of her eyes. There should have been a child . . . to say goodbye was the hardest thing in the world. This was his land. Even the soldier seemed to look insignificant now among them, was shut away by the door, pale and ineffectual. It was they who were strong, he thought. Touched hands, proud voices, strong words. Tied with cords that were stronger than death.

And they would bring him back.

Chapter 14

As he came down the steep scree towards the Lodge, the old man was caught up in a rush of stones and mud, and had to turn painfully on his side so that his hands could find something to grip. His palms were covered with mud, and a deep cut oozed blood through the dirt. There was no pain; he simply lay there for a moment, looking around him, far away in thought. Then, thinking with a wry smile of what Kate would say if he were to return in this mess, he continued slowly down to the burn and, bending, allowed the ice-cold snow water wash away the earth and blood.

Earth and blood, he thought to himself. Earth and blood - that was what the war had been about for him. In Africa, with long desert marches, endless miles and miles of sand, and that huge pitiless sun like a great oven whose coals flamed down as if in a kind of perpetual punishment, until the sudden fall of darkness. Sweat in one's sleep, the smell of bodies - dead and alive - and the engines of the flies, coming on everything like black scabs. Drink, when they could get hold of any, had been like a gentle death; it killed the pain for a little, dulled the sound of bombing, blurred the sight of towns on the horizon burning without reason. He drank to forget, so that the happenings of the coming day might be kept hidden in the darkness of the desert; he drank also to remember, to be able to see the dawn come through the glen, and a wood carpeted with bluebells, and the face of a girl at a cottage window.

Never for a single moment did he feel that he fought an enemy; for him, the enemy was one man, the personification of all that was evil, one who destroyed his own people as surely as he did Dan's own. And he did not come to this desert to fight, but stayed with his maps and his plans in a secret room somewhere in Germany. The men he saw dead, they were not enemies. Most of them were no more than boys, with whom he could easily have talked, and shared stories, and exchanged photographs of girls and wives and children. Of course he told these thoughts to no-one. How could he tell even his friends how he cried inside when he saw the white faces, the bodies that slept where the shells had blown their lives away. He cried because they would never see their homes again, just as surely as he cried for his own dead, the soldiers whose voices he had known, whose stories he had heard over and over again. The ones who had proudly shared with him the little tattered pictures of the girls they had left behind.

There was the Irishman, Connolly, who swore blind to all and sundry that he had been teetotal all his life but who would get roaring drunk whenever he got the chance and talked nothing but broad Irish Gaelic. Occasionally, he and Dan would attempt to converse in their native tongues, with such an outstanding lack of success that the others would be convulsed with laughter. Davidson, a Glaswegian, kept Dominic, a pet rat, in his pocket and brought it out at meal-times, saying that it had to be kept fit and well to survive this war as it had been a present from his wife. There were some pertinent comments about this from the company. In the end Davidson went out on a night patrol and did not return; he was never found, nor was Dominic.

He had letters sporadically from Catriona; never from his father. Sometimes he would write a few words at the top of a page, but never more - not that Dan had expected anything else. It worried him greatly to think that some of Catriona's letters were lost. When one arrived, he would open it with trembling hands. At the beginning he would laugh out loud at remarks in the letter, sharing them like a child with those around him, certain of their appreciation. After a time he stopped; as the months passed he was only too aware of the dangerous silence some of the lads were experiencing from the wives and girlfriends they had left behind. So occasionally he kept a letter all day, reading it avidly at night in the light of the lanterns. He wrote back to Catriona spasmodically. He would have no heart for it, the days rolling by in one long battle for water, for rest, for whisky, for peace; then one day he would wake up very early with a physical ache of longing for her, and he would write madly, telling her how much he loved her, assuring her that the war would soon be over and he would be home. Of the war in the desert he said nothing; he asked about the glen, about the farm animals, about the driving test she was planning to take soon. At times he really believed the war would end soon, but then it seemed to be stalemate and he would feel he was stuck there for ever and that he could not possibly go on.

It was during one such low time that he happened to be out alone and found the German. Of all his war experiences, this was easily the most vivid in his mind. He had gone out with Edwards, a Londoner with whom he had struck up a friendship. They had then gone in different directions. Dan had brought out his water bottle and put it to his lips - and then stopped dead. A man was lying on the ground near his feet, looking up at him; blood oozed from his chest, and his hands too were red with blood. Dan had heard shooting earlier, and now saw one of their own soldiers lying with his head half-buried in the sand. The German was breathing badly; his hands twitched and he tried to rise, but he was clearly badly wounded and could not move. All the time Dan was aware of his eyes fixed on the water bottle.

At first Dan stared stupidly at him; he could not, he thought, have been more than eighteen or nineteen. He saw the flies as they sizzled and boiled on his wounds, and the half-open mouth called out with thirst, but the noise that came out of it was a kind of rattle, the sounds of an old man. Dan kept staring at him in fascinated horror; he felt a fear beyond anything he had ever known. He had seen death, had even grown used to death, but this was something far worse, a land between two worlds which was like hell itself. But he did not leave; he was as it were locked together with the dying boy beneath his feet. And in the end he bent down, and with quaking hands tipped water feverishly between the gaping teeth, and saw the drops that were not swallowed run like liquid gold over unshaven cheeks and chin. There was a bad smell from the German's mouth and Dan longed to go; but he could not, he could not; he stayed, watching the eyes, listening to the throat as it began to utter the pathetic cries of a young child. *Oh God, let him die, let him die!* A hand suddenly reached out like a claw for his own, but he did not want to hold this hand; he did not want this man's blood on him. But he held it all the same; he did not know why, but it did not matter. Then, of all the strange things, he found himself singing softly the song his grandmother had sung to him long ago when he used to go and stay overnight up at Balree and would call out in the dark in fear. The Gaelic words came easily to his mind and he sang with assurance. He closed his eyes and he was singing for himself as well, for all that was beautiful and good, and somehow for a few moments the darkness was shut out, and a kind of peace came. There were still things to love and praise.

He opened his eyes and saw that the mouth had closed, the head had fallen away to one side and the terrible sound from the chest was ended. Edwards and another soldier were approaching, shouting to him and asking what the hell he was doing there; and Edwards had a bottle from which he thankfully accepted a slug.

He and Edwards were joking together, two days later, when they hit a mine. Etched in slow lightning, he saw Edwards' body coming down, torn apart. Dan had been on the outer side of the explosion and only one side of him caught the blast; an electric length of pain was injected into his left leg, and he was dimly aware of someone screaming - and then that it was himself - before the light was turned off and a bliss of blackness overtook him.

Dan woke in one of the field stations, seeing a woman's face swim before his eyes, and he was not sure if it was a dream. He drifted off into darkness again, and then the woman seemed to be speaking to him from a long way off. He felt desperately sick and wanted to be left in peace, aware of himself again being washed away by the tide of darkness. A long time later, or so it seemed, he opened his eyes and found himself in a large ward. The window was open and he could hear birds. Everything was very still and he lay there drinking in the cool air, and watching the sky which was the finest blue. There was a slight movement beside him and as he turned his head slowly he saw a young man sitting by the bedside, smiling, a white coat over thin arms.

'Hullo! You've had a long sleep, haven't you?'

He patted Dan's good leg and grinned.

'Well, the good news is that you'll walk again. We've had quite a time of it trying to save your leg - pretty smashed up it was when you came in here. But you'll get there OK now.'

'And what about the bad news?' asked Dan weakly, trying to raise himself and failing.

'A good deal of pain, I'm afraid. In your arm too. But you'll be going home soon - that should help! Not many days now.'

Going home! He couldn't take it in. He opened his mouth to ask 'why?, when?', but the doctor had moved on; and he lay back, wild with thoughts. It was so sudden, he hardly felt ready. He slept again, and in his dreams he was back at Achnagreine. The dream seemed to go on and on, sometimes Catriona was there, sometimes his mother, and sometimes he was back at Balree with his grandmother. Then he would be setting off for home all alone, trudging across the sand, with the sun like a cross on his shoulder. He would awake frightened and distressed and then, overjoyed, he would sleep and dream again.

At last they got him up and soon he was stamping around the wards, seeing those who had lost legs and arms, feeling their eyes boring through him as if in envy of the wholeness he still had. He felt almost guilty then, longing at times to be back among the lads he had known so well, the ones he had not said goodbye to. Amid all the sweat and blasphemy and cigarette smoke, they had shared a kind of terrible companionship, even love; they had cared about each other without ever putting it into words. He missed them. Ordinary men, come here to survive and go back together. One night he dreamed that he had found his way back to the camp to say goodbye, and all the lost dead were there. He saw each face, heard their voices and laughter, and in the dream he felt it was all right now; he could go home.

But it never happened - there were no goodbyes. One day he arrived in England after a long journey, and a huddle of people on the quay greeted the soldiers on a grey day of rain. There was black smoke over the flat land, and he felt nothing, nothing, just an emptiness inside him; or maybe, rather, a hard lump of poison, a knot of misery that never went away. Eventually he was on his way home at last, and he limped through the half-empty streets early one morning and waited nervously for a train that would take him north to Edinburgh. Everything seemed so quiet, so normal; suddenly he felt a kind of rage at these people who were going about their business, with nothing to worry them but their ration cards and coupons. How safe they were; they did not have to live with the smell of blood! He wanted to scream at the crowds on the station platform; he felt sick inside.

Once inside the train, he leaned his head against the side of the carriage, shutting his eyes and forcing himself to be calm and imagine the glen, and the river, and Achnagreine. And Catriona. *I must pull myself together*, he said to himself a dozen times, and as he came nearer to home, he somehow believed that a change would come over him, and he would find as it were the skin of his old carefree self lying waiting for him to put on again.

At long last he came to Abercree, yet still he felt nothing but emptiness inside. He could not face going any farther - he went past the Black Watch Inn and then turned back, with the thought that a drink or two might put some strength into him. He stood alone with his whisky in the corner of the bar. Someone was playing an accordion; all eyes were on the player and nobody took any notice of Dan, nor did he want to be noticed. He felt like a complete stranger, a dead man come back. Why would his hands not stop shaking? He slammed down his glass and ordered another drink. As he sat in a corner, other voices, other faces came into his mind. He saw the playing cards in Edwards' hands, heard Davy doing his well-worn impressions, saw Davidson feeding the rat Dominic pieces of cheese. All kinds of memories came rushing back, tiny things that he had grown used to from day to day as the bonds between them all had strengthened. He had a sickening feeling of having betrayed them all; should he not still be out there?

Suddenly he had a vivid picture of Catriona's face and knew a far sharper sense of betrayal. What was he doing here when she was up the glen waiting for him? He almost flung down his glass and made for the door; soon he was walking with his head down in the rain. There was no-one about and he knew the chances of a lift were slight. Well, he would walk. He crossed the old bridge that led towards the long miles of the glen road. In a short time he heard a car, but did not slacken his pace. The car stopped. It took him a moment to find the handle and fumble his way inside, and then to focus on the face of the driver.

It was Catriona.

Chapter 15

In the end it was all right. There *was* a way back. And eventually, after a long hard haul, she brought him there, carrying in her arms the pieces of him that were broken.

For many months he had an anger inside him that could be triggered like a gun. In the middle of the night he would waken up shouting, his body drowned in a sweat that seemed to come from the desert's own heat. There had been those early words of his father.

'Now you're back where you belong.'

And he had raged at the lie.

What do you know about it?, he said to himself, not once but many times. *You never saw them, did you? You never had to wonder if they'd be there the next day! And they're still out there getting blown to bits. No-one even remembers them, least of all the ones that sent them. They've got to stick it out while we live here nice and easy and talk about prices and markets, and worry about the weather. It's rotten to the core, that's what it is. Rotten!*

Rages like this wore him out. There was sand in all his clothes, but in the end nothing remained. Just a long expanse of desert in his mind, a place of silence for the ones he had lost.

Only Catriona saw it. She did not ask to be admitted there; but she called as it were from the outside, and with gentleness and patience brought him out from the grey walls in which he was imprisoned. Afterwards he wondered what would have happened to him if she had been other than she was; he did not like to speculate. Not once did she reproach him, nor turn aside from the anger he hurled at her; never at any time did she even mention the nights when he had not gone to bed but had sat at the fire, thunder in his eyes and a mouth foul with whisky. One night he had gone to bed early for a change, and then came down around midnight; she was sitting quietly mending his socks. He marvelled at her patience and forbearance. It was never in her nature to make a fuss about anything, he remembered after all the years. Nor did she ever try to tell him what to do. But there had been a single, remarkable exception.

One Saturday afternoon when he was sunk in a deeper depression than usual, she suddenly said:

'Dan, go and see the minister.'

He looked up, startled.

'And who is he?' he asked - he had not gone near the church since his return, and expected to hear it was a stranger.

'It's still John Maxwell,' she answered. 'He had to go away as a chaplain, but he was invalided out like yourself and he's back'.

Dan did not reply, but later in the evening he said, casually, that he would take a walk down to Drumbeg.

'Take the van, Dan,' was all she said.

But he replied that he felt like walking.

He never told anyone of his talk with John Maxwell that night. It had been in a way like rolling the years back, to that other time fifteen years ago when he was grieving for his grandmother and terrified of losing his mother. This man had offered him the road to faith then, and he had turned away. This time it was different, though; he was desperate, cold and dead inside. The sac of poison inside had to burst, or he was finished. He could not, could not go on living like this. He knew that and so did Catriona, for all she said nothing and bore everything.

No great light shone, he remembered. There seemed only to be enough light to see by, but as he walked home under a sky ablaze with stars, he felt for the first time a sense of peace, a kind of security he had despaired of ever knowing. He went in and found Catriona sewing; he said nothing but gave her a hug. And next morning he came down dressed not in his dungarees but in his good clothes, and she looked up with her eyes alight and they hugged each other hard again. One day, he thought, I'll

131

really come back to Achnagreine having laid the soldier I was in a grave far away.

And so it was that, always with Catriona's quiet help, his healing slowly began. She made him rest his leg as much as was possible and had him beside her in the warmth of the kitchen. She chatted to him about all kinds of things to take his mind off the war - about her driving, the time she had knocked over a pheasant and managed to slip it into the back of the van to make a rare addition to the meat ration; about the vegetable plot she had worked so hard on, and the family of rabbits she had watched very early one morning taking her carrots but didn't have the heart to chase away. She described how several children had started coming on Saturday mornings while he was away. She was teaching them to bake, and how to look after hens, and help with the lambing. And about the time a pine marten had come on to the window ledge one early morning and had tried to lick out an old honey pot she had left there.

He improved steadily under her constant care. He had relapses, times when he could have screamed, even at her, and wanted nothing but peace and quiet. He would bang the door as he went out; and, as he had done before, make for the wood or the ancient barrow. At times he found himself talking at her, trying to make sense of it all.

'I miss them all so much,' he would say. 'If only it hadn't ended as it did. Just to have had the chance to say goodbye . . . I just wasn't ready. I wish I could have gone back, just once.'

She came and leaned close to him and the scent of her hair was fresh and sweet, her hands gentle as she held his face and looked deep.

'You can't go back, Dan. It's finished. They're gone.'

And after a time the ghosts themselves began to die; like weak and flickering lights they burned out one by one - Edwards, Davy, Connolly, Davidson. He would never forget them but they ceased to haunt him; only from time to time in an unguarded moment a spasm of pain cut him like a knife.

The lambing in the spring played a big part in his healing. Dan could do a little by then, but he still could not walk far on the steep ground without the pain in his leg beginning to rage. Catriona helped with the work, and more than once he found she had got up while he slept, to help Johnny when things were especially busy. He felt her come back into the bed very early one morning, cold and shivering. He turned to face her, and ran his hands gently through the soft hair.

'Oh, there was one wee angel,' she whispered, her eyes dancing as she looked at him. 'Just legs made of jelly, footballers' socks on him - and something else, only you'll be mad if I say it.'

He shook his head lazily, smiling back at her. He was safely sleepy. 'He had such a look of yourself, Dan!'

He roared with mock anger and rolled over to grab her as they laughed together. Holding her, he then said shyly:

'Are you wanting lambs yourself, Catriona?'

She looked at him steadily, not blinking. Just nodded, and went on holding him. But no child came to them that summer or autumn.

In the winter something happened that was to change a great deal in their lives. Johnny Drummond was fixing some of the slates on one of the outhouses' roofs, and fell. The grass there grew sparsely in ground that was rock-hard with the frost, and it was his back that took the worst of the fall, for he had come down twisted; and he was a heavy man. So it was that Dan had to drag him upstairs; and on each step he remembered the times when his father used to find him as a child, fallen and with blood on his knees and roaring, and how the big arms had carried him. Now the positions were reversed; it was his back, his legs, that now had to bear the strain. They had, indeed, as it later proved, silently changed places, although neither knew it at the time. Dan was given the chains of office; it was his load now to bear. But all he thought about at the time was the agony his father must have endured on that long afternoon, an agony far deeper than any pain in his back - his fallen pride, his broken power.

Johnny lay in bed twisted and turned away, refusing both food and comfort; his eyes were black like a beast's, or so it seemed to Dan at the time. He never called them, never made any requests. And Dan pitied him and longed to say something to show his concern and, yes, his love; but no words came. Only his inner voice cried to the man who was his father and hoped he heard and understood. But aloud he said nothing; he felt helpless and frustrated and dumb.

All that winter it seemed to rage and batter at the windows as if reflecting the anger locked up in Johnny Drummond's head. Dan now had the farm to manage, so there was no longer any question of his accepting any outside work. So much to do, he thought at times almost despairingly; there was a hole in the barn roof and more than one of the dykes needed repairing; a blizzard came and three sheep were suffocated in the snow. He floundered around the fields wondering how he could ever cope with it all, how indeed his father had ever done it. At times he panicked and felt that he needed far more time - there was so much to learn; he and his father had worked together so little over the years. What he needed was for Johnny to become strong again. One evening, as Catriona was placing buckets inside the back door for the leaks and the rain was lashing against the windows, the doctor came. Sitting with them at the fire afterwards, he quenched that hope.

'No, Dan,' he said, 'that back of his is finished. He's had it fine and strong all these years - few around these parts could compare with him for sheer strength - but you can't go on putting that kind of strain on a back for ever. I'm afraid it just had to give in the end. He should have been slowing down over the years, you know, not lifting the kind of mountains he was.'

There was silence for a moment while Dan and Catriona digested this, and then the doctor added:

'I mean, he'll *walk* again all right, but he'll never do another lambing.'

'You haven't told him that, I hope?' Dan queried anxiously.

The man lifted his hands helplessly.

'He asked me to tell him the honest truth, Dan, and I owed him that - as a doctor and a friend. After all, he had to know sooner or later.'

'This was surely sooner,' Dan muttered half to himself, wishing fervently that there had been another way. So much had already been taken from him! Just to have had some hope would have make all the difference. He knew Johnny so well; certainly he had asked for the truth, but was it not, deep down, more likely to be told what he most wanted to hear?

Dan said no more to the doctor, who left soon after to face the storm. For a while they sat, in silence but for the clicking of Catriona's knitting needles.

'I'll get him dressed and help him down to the fire - make him feel a bit more normal' Dan said.

After a struggle, his father consented, and they sat listening to the storm for a while.

'Come with us to church tomorrow, father,' Dan then dared to suggest.

Johnny turned slowly towards him and the darkness in his eyes caused him to shiver.

'We'll make you comfortable in the back of the van; you'll be all right,' he continued.

'Ach, leave me alone, I'm finished,' his father said hopelessly.

Dan did not argue. What was there to say? He understood what his father meant. The last lightning had struck, and for him it seemed there was nothing to get up for any more.

'Father, let us help you back to bed,' Dan said at last when it was late and they were both tired.

Johnny did not reply; he just sat, his big arms hung over the chair. Catriona said goodnight and went upstairs. Dan lingered. He bent down beside the chair, his head lowered. Now, or perhaps never; what was it he wanted to say? Say it, say it! All the things. All the times they had passed by on the other side of one another, dumb beasts that had lost their speech. Far apart, locked in different worlds, yet forever joined.

Then: 'I see it, father. Don't think I don't understand. To be broken like that - in a single moment. To feel you can't go back, that there's nothing left. I can hardly bear it for you, and that's the truth. But maybe there's still a chance.'

His father turned his head sharply. Dan waited, half-expecting the mouth to fire at him as once it had done, to tear him in pieces. But there was the strangest hint of a smile and the eyes were wet.

'No, Dan, it's no use - it's the end for me. Maybe it's better this way than slowly going back, losing hold - I don't know. Anyway it's yours now; that was the way your brother wanted it; Achnagreine's your own. And there's no better place on earth, son, no place that could haunt a man more than this land'. He smiled and ruffled Dan's hair gently. 'Just promise me one thing - you'll never let this land go to an Englishman!'

Dan shook his head, laughing, but at the same time his throat was choked. He put his arms round his father and hugged him hard. When his voice returned, he managed to say:

'Aye, father, I promise!'

He helped the old man up to his room, and then went to his own, but did not light the lamp so as not to waken Catriona. Instead he went to the window and opened the curtains a little; he looked out at the thick waves of snow that came round in drifts and circles; already it had made a thick white covering. He was cold, but he did not want to sleep. Like a child he stood there, watching the endless world of fragments carried on the northern wind. It was beautiful; this land was always so beautiful.

He woke up early that Sunday morning. The frost had come and the skies were brittle blue. He turned over lazily and realised Catriona was not there. He would go back to sleep, he thought; it was warm and quiet.

'Dan!'

She was at the door in her nightdress, the pale oval of her face white against the dark hair.

'He's not here - not in the house! Oh Dan, where would he have gone?'

He got up quietly, although her words had shaken him. He held out his arms for her; she was shivering, and he could see her breath in the cold air. He nodded, searching her face.

'He knew, Catriona. You saw as well as I did that he worshipped only one thing in the end - take his land from him and you'd kill him - didn't we always know that? It was the same when mother was alive. Take his land from him,' he repeated, 'and you take his heart out. That's what happened, love; and no wonder!'

As he dressed quickly, he said to her 'Don't worry about breakfast for me. Go yourself to church. I'll more than likely be away for hours, but don't worry about me.'

She protested that at least he must have his breakfast, but he said he wasn't hungry. Down in the kitchen she put rolls and cheese in a bag and pressed them into his pocket.

'You'll at least take these. And you just look after yourself, Dan,' and she flicked his cheek with a finger, 'I don't want to lose you as well!'

They kissed and he went out, wrapped up against the cold.

He took one of the dogs, Donnie, with him and stood there in the yard, in that gold and blue breathless light which chipped the hills perfect and clear. How many hours had he been gone? Had he indeed ever gone to bed at all? He must have managed the stairs somehow, and perhaps gone out in the blizzard. Surely then they would have heard the old door on its grumbling hinges? He found tracks in the snow, but they were smothered, indistinct; there had been a good deal of fresh snow on top of them. But he could follow them all the same as they led down to the burn and across, and wound drunkenly up and on towards the edge of the wood. He reached there and lost the prints among the thick trunks of the alders and pines where only odd freckles of snow lay.

He went on, to the very edge of the wood. Far beyond, the empty moor suddenly came to life when six greylag geese heard him and flew upwards with the sound of bagpipes in their shivering wings. But here there was nothing. Across the expanse of snow that was a foot deep not one living creature had passed. It was an unbroken land, untouched, and for a moment Dan only gazed over it, marvelling, forgetful of why he had come. In the distance was the first of the lochs, shining blue and deep, a skin of ice reaching out across the few yards of its surface nearest to the shore. It was like a stained glass window set in the holy sanctuary of this wild horse-shoe between hills. It was moving beyond all words.

He stepped back and wondered *Where now?* The tracks he had followed, they must certainly have been his father's; but beyond the edge of the trees, where could they go? Suddenly he remembered the ancient mound; he had not looked there. So he went down over the hard ground and the deep layers of frozen leaves, and once more surveyed the glen below, and Achnagreine. But here, where the first men had made their abode, there was nothing but the whispering of the tall pines and the quick flight of a tiny wren. He was wrong again. Where would his father have gone? He must think, he must think. How far could he have got in the snow? But then he recalled the hours after frost came, and how there would have been light from the snow and clear skies; the old man would have found his way all right. It came to him then as distinctly as any picture and he nodded, breathed the word, and was off at once up through the wood and on by the other side, the western edge, towards the scrawny neck of the Tor.

Sure enough he found tracks, weaving across the white, frozen land. On and up he went, searching, searching. Then all at once he was at the cave, that haven of men before history; and the search was abruptly over. There lay Johnny, his face to the sky; and as Dan bent to feel uselessly for the pulse he knew already he would not find, he saw that the eyes were closed and the mouth still, not set in anguish. It was as though he might have been sleeping.

Dan sat down beside his father. He did not feel that he should weep. Indeed, a taut string inside him seemed to break; almost as if something rose up and was gone, and there was left an emptiness; but he did not mourn. He sat unmoving while his mind ranged far, back over the years it went, seeking for answers to many questions. Had Johnny ever really known happiness? Perhaps, perhaps. In the days when he himself was an infant, when his mother was still young, and sorrow had not yet touched them? But then the wounds - they had come, one upon another, until it must surely have seemed that God was punishing him. And always there had been the land. The legacy of Alan, Johnny's father - a few poor acres of sheep farm on the rough slopes of Beinn Dobhran. Acres strewn with streams and boulders, scant enough pasture for the beasts, a place exposed to the fury of the winter winds. Could this man really have given his heart to such a land? Or had it simply taken possession of him, stolen him away from those who loved him, and in the end led to his death in this lonely place?

The fear then came to Dan that he too was in the same danger; might he not be swept away by the same obsession? After all, the same blood flowed in his veins; could it be that he, now that he was master of Achnagreine, would turn fallow and in the end be overcome? *Let it not be so!* He breathed the words like a prayer. He whispered them again - 'let it not be so!' He had seen what his father had done to them all, year after year, regretting only when it was too late. Many a time Dan had sworn that he would never forgive, never forget the years of betrayal.

Yet forgive he did - the old man whose grey head he had held last night and kissed, who had at last in a moment become real, become his father. What if he had not managed to say the words of sympathy, of reconciliation? How different it would have been for him at this moment if he had not!

They buried Johnny three days later beside his wife Rena and his parents, John Maxwell conducting the service with sincerity and simplicity. To Dan's surprise, for Johnny had had few close friends, most of the glen came to the funeral. Perhaps they had found him hard to understand; but they had respected his integrity, and he was one of them. In the hush after the coffin had been lowered into the earth, the single fluting note of a curlew was heard, high and sad. Dan lowered his head, feeling an overwhelming sense of peace. There was nothing to add.

Tomorrow he would begin again. Perhaps there would soon be children to run about the yard and help with the feeding of the orphan lambs. How blessed they would be - Catriona would give them the world!

After all the people of the glen had departed, he and she sat in deep peace together, looking out at the darkness rolling down, avalanche after avalanche, from Beinn Dobhran. Dan had no idea how long they sat there. And as they went at last to bed, he looked up at the stars burning high above, and the ring of dark hills all around, and he knew he had come home.

Chapter 16

It began to snow. Small crumbs of wet ice at first, that touched the hands and broke into water. But then larger and whiter flakes came circling down, and Dan felt the cold and the dark weigh down upon him. He knew that he should go back to the shelter of the house; the warm orange glow from the kitchen window drew him; but he did not want to go back. This might be his last day and he did not want it lost. If he went down to the barns, Kate would be sure to come out, tell him he would catch his death of cold, scold him as if he were a child, tell him it was time he took his pills. No, he was not going to go inside.

Now the snowflakes were thatching the wild white hair, so fast they fell. He began to make his way down to what had been the ruins of the old Lodge - now splendidly rebuilt for the new owner. His sight was not good and he slipped on the wet ground beneath the trees; he stopped for a moment to recover his breath and then found the old path. His thoughts were far away; as he came around the side of the house, it was the Lodge as it had been long ago that he was seeing; his heart could still miss a beat as he recalled that day of horror in his boyhood when the flames had taken it. And his grandmother, she had seen it all; why had nobody listened to her?

He was startled out of his reverie by the sight of the figures on the lawn, a large, gleaming vehicle parked nearby. Who were these people? He did not want to disturb them; in some confusion he turned away. But one of the figures detached itself from the little knot of people, and a clipped English voice said briskly:

'I'm terribly sorry, but this is private property.'

Dan thought that he did not sound the least bit sorry!

'I really must ask you to go.'

The old man looked closely at the speaker. He saw a tall man with a moustache, fine clothes and a cravat beneath his jacket.

'I had no idea there was anyone at the Lodge,' Dan said in bewilderment, speaking so quietly that the other man had to bend towards him to hear the words.

'Ah well, yes, my name's Turner. We bought this place recently, intend to run it for shooting parties - Germans, Americans, you know the sort of thing. But now I really must ask you to leave; it's private property and I'm sure you'll understand that we can't have everyone who's passing simply walking over the place.'

Dan looked at him, confused, trying to focus on what he was saying, trying to take in the words. He could not think of anything to say. Anyway it was too late; who would listen to him, what did he have to say that anyone wanted to hear? His time was past; all decisions were out of his hands, everything slipping away. Like the trout in the burn, he thought; where once he had guddled them in the deep pools, now they would slip through his fingers. He could not hold on to anything any more. He turned slowly away, not knowing where he should go. The man Turner had returned to the other figures on the lawn, and they all moved towards the Lodge. The snow was beginning again.

He went down in the end towards the road, past where he remembered the flower beds used to be; he would go along the road a little way and then up through the trees, skirting the Lodge. And then on up to Achnagreine - as his grandmother had done, when she was banished from the Lodge all those years ago. His journey in memory - the thoughts of the past that had come crowding in on him all through today - where had he left off? His mind wandered so easily! He must think; he must return to complete the memories of the years. Now he remembered! The death of his father.

The years since then, and they were many, had been good. Hard, but good. He and Catriona had never had a child. How much that had broken her, and for so long, nobody would ever know. How often he used to pray that a child might come! And for all her secret tears, the prayer had never been answered. There had been no small hand to lead to the places they loved.

For all that, Catriona had not turned away; several small figures could often be seen making their way up the brae to Achnagreine over the years. One or two had lost their fathers in the war; one belonged to a single mother who worked hard to provide for her child; others came simply because they loved Catriona. She was an angel to them all, he thought; she would turn the kitchen into a playroom for them, and when he came home he would find her baking with them, or modelling with plasticine, the floor covered with a jungle of animals. It used to break his heart to see her say goodbye to the little party as they set off down the road again, waving at every turn. She did not once complain; but he could feel his chest contract with pain for her.

He had taken up the fiddle again. He recalled how he had thrown it down in frustration at around the age of ten, and it had been banished to the attic along with paintings and old chairs and a rocking-horse Johnny had once made for his brother Andrew. He had got it down and dusted off the layers of time, and polished up the wood that was like the colour of a chestnut newly broken out of its shell. He smiled as he remembered how Catriona had winced at his first notes; she had laughed and said the dogs would start howling if he went on playing like that. So he removed himself and the fiddle to a spare room and practised for an hour each evening. Then, when she had at last admitted he was becoming quite good, he dared to ask the boys up. New Year had been the first time, he recalled; after that it became a monthly event, when they produced a lively medley of marches, strathspeys and reels, and an evening of sheer enjoyment. Word got around, and from time to time they were invited to play at a ceilidh down in Drumbeg. Not, of course, for money; nobody had bothered about that in those days. And then he had persuaded Catriona to begin singing again. For a while she did nothing about it, but then one day she came in with a whole pile of music and dumped it on the floor beside him, having been to Abercree to spend the day with her folks.

'Well, it's your own fault,' she said laughing. 'Don't say you weren't warned.'

He had put on weight and blamed it on her baking. They were at ease with one another, always with so much to share, happy in each other's company. There were times he used to see her like his mother - the gentle joy in small things, and yet the stubbornness that could at times lock him out and render him helplessly weak. Never did he understand her fully, nor what it was exactly that he longed for and found in her. It was the same, in a way, with the land; all the parts shifted and changed in the light - you could never say what the whole meant, could not capture the words that would paint it and set it fast, as it were framed. But you found yourself going back and back again; the thirst inside you would be quenched for a moment but returned, stronger, different; and the water was never the same twice, nor the colour of the light.

Sometimes he had to admit to a measure of selfish relief that they had no children. How could he ever have shared her? And yet . . . and yet the heaviness of it weighed him down too. Not only because of the wound in her which he knew would never heal, but because there would be no boy to follow him at Achnagreine, to take the reins of this land, and learn to ride and steer it. It was at times like a knife in him to think they would be the last in this place.

The people of the glen were dying too. He saw it year in, year out; faces he had known from early childhood, now gone; folk who had had their corners of hillside and were written into the names of each homestead - it was as though a river had swept them away. But it was not simply the loss of the old which caused him pain; it was the loss, in a different way, of the younger ones who were taking their place. When had the changes begun? When was it that they had started to lose their heritage,

144

to prefer the songs of America to those of their own race? When had they turned from their own language? Not a single child now could understand Gaelic; the songs lived only with the old, who could no longer sing them. When had it all begun, Dan asked himself again; why was it that nobody, including himself, had seemed to notice or take any action? He could not think, could not understand. Now it was too late; he was too old and too tired. One thing he did know; some changes had come about through the intrusion of alien ways of life - by television, and by people of other lands. But there was more; there was a change within the people themselves.

One year they had found gold, on the other side of the glen, in one of the larger burns. A nugget of gnarled yellow metal that had quickly brought people eager to try their hand at finding riches for themselves. They came with caravans and loud music, and they threw their rubbish by the roadside. One night they returned drunk from down the glen, and young Iain from Camus Lurgan was killed when their van careered into a rock-face. Dan remembered how the whole glen had mourned. Four weeks later, though, the gold hunters had moved on - it was said that not enough gold had been found to make even a wedding ring.

After that, a kind of normality had returned for a while. However, there were always new dangers, always more erosion of the old way of life. Oh, he knew fine that these were the conclusions of an old man, one who clung to the familiar patterns of life; but were these not the best? When, for example, had the young ones ceased to find fascination in the land, in all the beauties of the glen which had delighted himself and his friends? Did any of the boys even know these days how to guddle trout? He could not think of a single one.

His memory was not what it used to be; he could no longer remember dates and times other than things that had happened long ago. There had been the new hotel built at the mouth of the glen, and a new music had come, beside the voice of the river. Then there had been the dam up at Loch Lurgan, to bring electricity. It had been good to have the light - how his mother would have appreciated the freedom from the daily tyranny of cleaning the row of paraffin lamps! But in the end the dam had stood there, cold and sharp and alien, a concrete wall incongruous among the hills. Had that perhaps been one of the things that had turned the thoughts of so many to making money, to acquiring fancy houses and fast cars? There was a day, he thought, when it would never have crossed one's mind to notice what kind of a house anyone had. We were all equally poor, but our lives were rich, rich and satisfying in spite of all the hardships.

There was another thing. When was it that people had started locking their doors? Had this, at one time unheard of in the glen, perhaps started when people had begun to turn away from the church? Nowadays it was half empty! In the old days, everything had stood open: barns, houses and coalsheds. Loads of potatoes or peats, yes, and parcels from the grocer - or indeed the jeweller - could have lain for a week at the side of the road; nobody would have touched them. The honesty of the glen folk had been proverbial. How well he remembered the time his father, tired after a long day's work, had insisted on walking all the way down to Drumbeg one night to return an extra shilling he had been given in change by the postmaster! There was nothing unusual in that incident, he mused. But now the character of the people was different.

He decided he must stop these ramblings, and go on with his journey through memory. What was to be gained by an old man's opinions, now that nobody listened to him any more? He thought back to the time when he had begun to be aware of growing old . . . tired and old. He fell asleep in front of the fire after supper, when the wireless was on; he would even doze again after Catriona had wakened him with a cup of tea. Catriona. She too had grown older, her hair turned grey and her face filled with the lines of the years; but still his

Catriona, the one he loved. Her laugh was still the same, her eyes the deep pools which he could never quite fathom.

He had begun to need more help with the sheep - more than the normal assistance from neighbours at the dipping and shearing. He had had to cut the size of his flock; and it hurt him like a wound. Time was biting; the winds were stronger, Beinn Dobhran steeper. And then all of a sudden Catriona fell ill. It was such a shock to him that he felt as though the house had been struck by lightning. Oh, she had been ill before, of course, but she had always struggled on, and in a day or two she would be as right as rain. This time it was different. He came home to a cold and silent house, with only the old clock breaking the silence in the kitchen. It was in the middle of the busy lambing season too; at times she went from his mind as the hours went by in hard work, and tiredness pounded in his head. Then he returned to the house to find nothing but the dogs whining at the fireside. He would go up and sit with her, even at times when she was sleeping; and he would offer to go for the doctor, but she would say it was only a pain in her chest and she would be fine after some rest. In the early mornings he often lay awake by her side as she turned restlessly, un-comfortably, asleep but not rested. And he would say to himself, 'Next week she'll be better; she'll be out with me to see the new lambs, to feed the two small orphans in the barn.'

Then one night he came in and she heard him and turned her face to the light. It was no longer pained, he noticed, and her eyes were shining.

'Are you better, Catriona?' he asked with rising hope, hushed, and kneeling by her bedside. But she had just shaken her head, smiling.

'Dan, tell me a story,' she had said unexpectedly, her voice sleepy, half-muffled by the pillow. He looked away out of the window at the moon over Beinn Dobhran, searching his mind for a story that would give her pleas-ure. They had done this together many a time, mostly in

147

the early summer mornings when the sun woke them and they could not get back to sleep. So many had been told; he must find a new one. Then it came to him - a story from his grandmother, from almost as far back as he could remember, in the days when the road up to Balree had seemed to go on for ever.

'All right,' he said gently, stroking her hair which was splayed all over the pillow. 'Close your eyes and think of the first lochan beyond the wood, away up on the shoulder of Beinn Dobhran.

'There was once a house there, long long ago; even the stones of it are gone now. But a young lad lived there, with his folks who struggled to scrape a living from that poor soil. One winter it was so cold that the loch froze solid. The skies cleared and the light was clear as glass. Anyway, the wee boy had always longed to skate. But they would never have had enough money to buy him skates; he knew that fine, and it made him very sad. Soon the ice would melt again and his chance would be lost, he thought. What could he do? One night he thought of a lassie he had always had a liking for; she lived in a fine house down in Drumbeg, and her parents were rich. Surely she would have skates! Next morning, off he went down to her house and shyly knocked at the door; he asked her, and sure enough, she had skates. So back she went with him to the corrie, and he watched impatiently by the lochside while she showed him how to skate. But as she went close to the far edge of the lochan - crack! The ice broke, and she fell into the freezing water and was lost from view. The poor boy was grief-stricken; his mother and father were both away at the croft and nobody was near at all. There was nobody to help and he could not even swim. And do you know what he did? He just crouched there by the side of the loch and cried - hour after hour, until the evening came and it grew cold. And he never stopped crying and his eyes were so full of tears that he couldn't see what was happening to the ice. But in the end all the tears melted it and turned the water warm! Suddenly the wee girl rose to the surface and cried

148

out for him to help her to the shore. And happy he was indeed. Even to this day they say that lochan will never freeze for the sake of the wee boy.'

He looked at her closely as he finished; her breathing was soft and easy, and he thought she had fallen asleep. But she opened her eyes and said softly:

'Thanks, Danny.' In a moment she added, smiling up at him, 'and now, a psalm; sing me a psalm.'

'Which one?' he asked.

'What but the 23rd?' she answered. 'The shepherd's psalm.'

He got up from the bedside so as to be able to sing more easily, and began:

'The Lord's my shepherd . . .,' but she stopped him at once.

'No, no, in Gaelic - it's so much better in Gaelic.'

So he sang the whole psalm, the words coming back to him without effort. When he had finished, he knelt again by the bed and saw that this time she really was asleep.

He did not dare move lest he should waken her, so he slept on the chair beside the bed, in his working clothes. He was cold during the night, for there was a hard frost, so he woke early, long before dawn, but there was light in the room, a light that came through the uncurtained windows and drew from the shadows the chest of drawers, the clock, chairs, and a painting of his mother's over the bed. He looked first into the yard; something fell from the little shelf beside the bed as he brushed it with his elbow; there was a clicking sound from below and he saw three roe deer, sculpted in velvet, leaping away into the field.

Then, very quietly, he bent down towards Catriona and saw her still lying as she had lain the night before, the marble light etching her whole face. But now she was no longer breathing.

A black cloud crossed his mind as he re-lived the utter desolation of that time; he could feel the knot of bitterness which had come to lodge inside him, the emptiness and loneliness nothing could assuage. A whole year, he remembered, had been filled with that bitterness - a year in which he had silently fought his own battle, allowing no-one else to come near or comfort - not even John Maxwell, although he had stood by quietly all the time, waiting to help. He had lived in a kind of daze, eating and sleeping when he needed to, working on - Achna-greine, his sanctuary and his all. His heart was like a stone; every place she had loved he could not, would not see, and he shut out of his mind. On the Sabbath he could not go to Drumbeg, for her face would be there before him. The words of her death were cut from cold stone in the churchyard; how could he ever bear to see them? He might as well have been dead, he told himself often; what was left for him here any more?

The months went on, arid and bare, until one day a little boy came running up the track, legs stocky, hair tousled straw, a little bunch of primroses clutched in his hand. He burst out:

'These are for Catriona!'

And the cold war was over, the dam at last burst. He bent down to the small head, put his arm gently round the shoulders, and cried. Cried for himself and for his dead, wooden heart, and for Catriona who had been for him the stream through which all his joy, his laughter and song, had flowed. But the world, he saw then, had not ended. He saw her in the faces of the flowers, smiling, as in the wren-bright eyes of the little boy who had loved her too.

And from that day he had allowed the blood to flow back into his veins, had allowed friends to come near him, had gone back to church and found a spark of faith again. Slowly, healing had begun. In a sense, the darkness did not grow any less, and the loneliness would be there always; but the small lights along the way began to make it easier to bear. As the years went by, there was fiddle music again at Achnagreine; and old friends came back, to share good talk round the fire in the evenings. He needed someone to help in the house; that was when

Kate came, with her son Roddy. Although the boy was strange and liked best to be on his own, it was good to have him about the place. As for Kate, her back was strong and her sight far better than his own, and she was good at the farm work. At first she was quiet and withdrawn, and when they sat at meals she hardly said a word, and sometimes her eyes seemed to flash at him as if she was nervous. Perhaps, he thought, she had heard stories of him, after his year of silence and anger? But maybe it was not that; maybe it was that she was self-contained, confident. She seemed to fear nothing; she made decisions quickly and stood by them. She grew frustrated by his slowness, and in the end he let her go off up to the top fields, while he himself worked away at the dykes down to the track, where he had peace and time.

Then when last winter came he had felt the cold as never before. He would lie awake in bed, listening to the wind, becoming fanciful, his eyes seeing in the half-light his mother and father and Andrew . . . and Catriona - always Catriona. The photographs that were fading.

Dan had come full circle. He climbed wearily up through the wood and saw Achnagreine ahead of him, on the little ridge. Now he was tired and the darkness coming fast. It would be good to sit by the fire again.

He did not see the deer fence until he was only a few steps from it. Towering over him by several feet, it seemed in his imagination a giant that stood in his way. Confused, he stood looking at it, his eyes searching for a way of climbing, but the mesh stretched up, shining and impregnable, held by the posts as if by a line of sentries. Maybe the gaps in the mesh would be wide enough to hold his feet? He went forward, reached up stiffly with both hands outstretched, placed his left foot unsteadily on the wire; then he swung up with his right. When it came to keeping both hands taut in that position, however, his strength failed; he attempted to step back but instead fell backwards, badly twisting his ankle. He tried to move but could not; he could only crouch there, on the ground that was covered partly with snow, partly with the mixed leaves of autumn, now frozen - leaves of birch, alder and rowan.

He turned round to look at the Lodge, his eyes just making out the empty shape of the lawns; nobody left there now. Hopelessly he shouted for Kate; his voice was lost in the wind. Flurries of snow came and went; how cold it was! He began to shiver uncontrollably. He closed his eyes and listened to the bleating of sheep and lambs in the distance. It grew darker still and now he could see nothing, nothing but the glow of the light of Achnagreine through the wire of the fence. He wished then with all his being that he could go home, home to the light, to the place of his people. But he could not get up now; he could not move an inch. Sleepy, he turned on to his side and curled up in an effort to keep warm.

After a long time he heard a voice. His heart leapt. It was Catriona, of course; she had come to find him! He talked to her, and asked her to take him home...

Chapter 17

The funeral was over. Kate had found the service strange, the long psalms tedious. The minister had spoken of a seed having to die in order for life to be born; she had found her thoughts wandering. A scattering of glen folk, most of them old, had walked away afterwards, some with sticks, some arm-in-arm with others. She walked quickly past them. Her shoes were dirty from standing in the graveyard; it was thawing fast and the trees were dripping. She must get back to the farm.

How dreary the kitchen was! It needed some bright new furniture, a better rug at the fireplace. She looked round for just a moment and then, her heart beating fast, went up the stairs two at a time and into Dan's room. Her hands trembled. She had seen the envelope in his spidery handwriting; here it was at last.

On the outside she saw the word 'Daniel'. What was this? Certainly a mistake - he had been confused for the last while, of course. She tore it open and began to read the single sheet of paper, her lips moving fast over the words:

My dear Daniel,

I have at last found your address and have arranged for this letter to be sent on to you when I am gone.

Many years ago when I was studying in Glasgow and you were just a little boy, I loved your mother. It is even possible that you still remember me from that time. In the end I left to come back to this glen and my own people. Before I went, I left behind for you the gift my own brother had given me when he went to the war, a set of toy farm animals. That was all a long time ago. But now I want to do what may seem a very strange thing - I want to leave you something else - this farm, Achnagreine, and its land.

It is the thing of most value that I have in this world, not because of its riches or a soil that will bring in much money, but because it is a precious piece of land, to me more precious than gold. Your grandfather was a sheep farmer in another place in the Highlands, and I believe you have inherited his love of the land. Perhaps you even remember from all those years ago how you loved the stories of this glen I used to tell you, and how you would say you wanted only to farm the land. You were as a son to me then, Daniel, and I have had no son since.

I do not want these fields to die, nor do I want their use to be changed. I ask you to come here, and your sons after you, to live in this place, to find in these fields both the living and the dead, to guard the land.

There's a new rowan tree I planted by the barn last year where one grew long ago - see that it grows good and strong!

May you always be blessed in this place.

Dan Drummond